CRYBABY BRIDGE

K. Wiley Sider

ISBN: 0692497196
ISBN 13: 9780692497197
Library of Congress Control Number: 2015912037
Devilwood Press, Ellicott City, Maryland

Some people live in places that don't have a name. They live outside a particular town or near the location of the closest post office or landmark. Some roads don't even have names. They're rural routes or county roads that have only numbers. For many people in the area, their address says "Someplace," though they were as far away from there as they were from anywhere else. But they needed to belong to somewhere, so some land-management official in some office somewhere in the state declared that this little piece of someplace needed to be called something. But to everyone who lived there—everyone who knew the truth—it was the middle of nowhere.

The interesting thing about living in the middle of nowhere is that all kinds of things happen there that nobody knows about.

ONE

Krissy

Cicadas sing. Most people think they chirp like crickets. But every few years, they come out of the ground and sing. And sometimes, if you listen for a really long time, they can hypnotize you.

They were singing to Krissy the day she went to Crybaby Bridge. They sang for her as she watched a dirty old baby doll somebody had hung in the tree sway in the breeze. After a time, Krissy began to sway too, in perfect time with that dead doll.

She didn't even care that her fart nugget brother, James, and his friends were probably yucking it up and making fun of her the way they usually did. She was showing them how brave she was by going to Crybaby Bridge all by herself...well, almost by herself, since James had to give her a ride on his handlebars, but she was standing there by herself, and she didn't even look back once.

She wouldn't look at the house that was set off from the road a bit just before the bridge either. But that didn't mean she wasn't brave, because nobody looked at that house if he or she could help it, even if it was an ordinary kind of house. Krissy tried to stare at it out of the corner of her eye, but that made her eyes water and her head hurt, so she moved her head just a little bit so that she was sort of looking past it and not really at it.

See, it wasn't anything to cry about. Just some plain old cement-block house with a bunch of weeds in the yard...and a ten-foot-high chain link fence around it...a fence with no gate...just a long unbroken stretch of aluminum fence...keeping people out...or something in.

Krissy really didn't care about that dumb baby doll hanging from the tree, even if it did look like it was swinging by itself. She didn't even care about the stink coming from Piss Creek, which probably had a real name even though only grown-ups knew what it was. Kids just called it Piss Creek because it stank so bad from the pig farm up the road. And maybe because the senior football players peed on the freshmen and then made them jump into it before they could be on the team.

Last year a junior varsity running back fell in and got really, really sick from all the pig pee and almost died. James tried to be funny and said he got man-gina, but Krissy knew it was called meningitis from listening to Mom, who worked at the hospital.

Even in her ten-year-old brain, Krissy figured there had to be a lot more than just piss in that water for some kid to get that sick, so she planned to steer clear from then on.

She was still a little worried, though. It was way hot and the stink coming off the creek was way bad. There had to be a breeze because that dumb baby doll was swinging and it seemed to be blowing the smell right at her on purpose. Krissy pulled her T-shirt over her nose and hoped she couldn't get meningitis from smelling.

That just made it hotter and harder to breathe. Krissy's eyes began to close and she was just about to doze off when a rock came sailing past her. It was so fast that she didn't even hear it until it hit the front door of the house with a loud clang. She thought it was a gunshot at first until she saw the dent the rock had made in the door.

Krissy stood stock-still, held her breath, and stared straight at that faded blue door with its new big dent.

And then it opened.

Krissy knew even before it actually opened that someone was opening it. Maybe there was a creak, or maybe she saw the doorknob turn, but whatever it was, Krissy knew someone...or something...was coming out. She wasn't sticking around to say "Hi, how are ya?" so with a tiny stumble over one of that darn tree's roots, Krissy took off like a shot.

Just in front of her she could hear her stupid brother laughing his stupid head off with his stupid friends as they ran to their bikes. Just behind her Krissy didn't hear anything at all, which just about creeped her out since anyone else would have hollered their heads off at the sight of a brand-new dent in their door.

By the time she reached the road, her brother and all but one of his friends were on their bikes, hooting and hollering while pedaling furiously down the road. One of the boys, though, a pimply sixth grader named Mason, was kneeling in the dirt trying to work his bike chain back around whatever that flat wheel-looking thing was called. Krissy ran past him and shot him a dirty look. She wanted to kick him or at least his bike, but she didn't dare in case he was the kind who'd kick her back. Instead, she made sure she kicked up as much dust as she could as she ran past.

It took Krissy only a minute to make it around the corner where James and his friends, minus Mason, had stopped on their bikes and were looking back over their shoulders. Krissy knew better than to think they were at all concerned about her, so she just ran on by. James glared at her as she passed.

"Where's Mason?" he barked.

Krissy adopted a look of nonchalance, which was pretty darn hard running and with a mean stitch growing in her side. "Boogeyman got 'im," she panted and then kept on running.

"Shit'all," she heard James mutter, which for darn sure she was going to tell their mother about. "Go on and get 'im."

Krissy, casually running and all, didn't need to look behind her to know that one of James's toadies was most likely pedaling off to do as he was bid.

Without a set of handlebars to sit on and that mean stitch still growing, Krissy veered a sharp right and left the blacktop to cut across Mr. Harper's hay field on her way home. Luckily for her, he hadn't cut his hay yet, and she was able to hide among the tall stalks of grass. Where the field bordered the far side of Mr. Harper's house, Krissy crouched down further so as not to get shot just like that stupid kid who thought it would be funny to tip Mr. Harper's cows and ended up with a face and shoulder full of buckshot. Krissy's mom had said he looked like a pizza with extra pepperoni when he came into her emergency room. Krissy knew all about every person who came into the emergency room; even though Krissy's mother wasn't a nurse, she was the lady who made sure that everyone had insurance before they were seen by a doctor.

Thoughts of a lifetime with a pepperoni pizza face spurred Krissy on faster and faster until she found the fence that bordered the hay field. Krissy wiggled through it and then made her way through the growing stands of corn to the other fence that marked the edge of the dirt drive that ran between the fields to her house. There was a break in that fence, so Krissy only needed to step over it and she was home.

Even though they lived in farm country with their driveway bearing an actual street name, Krissy's family had only a tiny little yard surrounding their small farmhouse. Just past the yard were acres and acres of weedy soybeans and cornfields that once belonged to Krissy's grandfather, who had sold everything off to pay back taxes. Once all the land was gone, Grandpa Nate decided to go crazy and checked himself into the Spring Haven Mental Hospital. Every week or two, Krissy and her family visited him. For a crazy man, he seemed awfully happy there.

Of course, none of this was going through Krissy's mind as she slowly stomped up the front steps, little plumes of light brown dust announcing her arrival. She wasn't thinking about very much at all as she let the screen door slam behind her, which brought out her grandmother, who wasn't really her grandmother but rather Grandpa Nate's third wife, Naomi. Her mind was completely blank when she looked up to see Grandma Naomi's mouth working wordlessly as she emitted soft, shushing sounds. Grandma Naomi couldn't talk after having had part of her tongue, jaw, and all of her voice box removed after a lifetime of smoking had left her with no teeth and cancer of the mouth and throat. Krissy still understood her even if everyone else pretended not to.

"I will, I will," Krissy muttered as Grandma Naomi silently insisted she clean up in the bathroom and not track any more dust into the house. Grandma Naomi followed her upstairs and took Krissy's dirty clothes away for washing. Too tired to stand up, Krissy sat in the bathtub and let the cool shower rinse the dirt away. Her reverie was cut short when Grandma Naomi abruptly turned the water off and tossed a towel onto Krissy's head.

"All right, all right," Krissy grumbled as she climbed out of the tub. She quickly dried off and then put on the clothes that Grandma Naomi had brought in.

When she was dressed, Krissy went into the kitchen where Grandma Naomi was chopping vegetables for the pot roast she was making for dinner. Without being told, Krissy picked up a vegetable peeler and began to peel carrots. Grandma Naomi smiled at her, and then the two lost themselves to their silent tasks.

Krissy was so caught up in her work that she didn't even notice James standing in the doorway. He was even dirtier than she had been and he was pinching his bottom lip between the knuckles of his fingers, something he did when he was really scared or really in trouble.

"You better clean up," Krissy warned him, feeling somewhat sure that Grandma Naomi would back her up.

James looked at her as if seeing her for the first time. "Where's Mason?" he asked, this time in a tone that sounded like he hoped Krissy had the answer.

"Well, about an hour ago he was tryin' to put his bike chain back on," Krissy said lightly as she stirred milk and sour cream into the mashed potatoes that would be put into the oven to bake with the roast.

"Where did he go after that?"

"How should I know? I ain't his babysitter." Krissy affected an irritated shake of her head that mirrored her mother's.

James continued to stare at her. "Are you sure?" he asked, again hoping she'd give him the answer he needed.

"Am I sure what?" Krissy gave her brother a blank look.

"Are you sure you saw him fixin' his bike?" James's voice sounded a little shaky, but Krissy was too tired of the conversation to notice.

"I guess." She shrugged. She was about to ask why when Grandma Naomi noticed dirty James standing in her clean kitchen and shooed him out with a wave of her dishtowel.

Krissy didn't give any more thought to Mason until the phone rang halfway through dinner. Everyone stopped eating for a moment and stared at one another in surprise. No one ever called during dinner unless it was a real emergency.

"Well," Krissy's mother, Ellen, huffed as she tossed her paper napkin onto the table, "I can't imagine who could be calling at this hour." Her chair scraped loudly across the wooden floor as she pushed away from the table and went into the kitchen to answer the phone.

Krissy's father, Frank, just grunted and then resumed shoveling his food into his mouth with mechanical precision.

Krissy turned to look at James, who stared at the opening to the kitchen with the most unlikely expression on his face. Krissy wasn't quite sure, but it looked like James was terrified.

"Sorry, Jen, but Mason's not here...are you sure? Well, hold on and I'll ask him." With her hand over the mouthpiece, Ellen leaned around the doorway and whispered loudly, "James, do you know where Mason is?" Krissy turned back to see James's face turn a chalky white. He shook his head slowly.

"Huh uh?" he answered. Ellen didn't seem to notice James's odd reaction and returned to the kitchen.

"No, he hasn't seen him. Well I realize it's after six. Did you try Peggy? Oh...he's not? Well, I don't know what to tell you...I'm sure he'll show up soon. I'll give you a call if I hear anything. All right then. Bye." Ellen returned to the table with an irritated shake to her head. "Well, you'd think people could keep track of their own kids," she sniffed, and then sat down to finish her meal.

Krissy stared at James as he started to choke on his pot roast. Without breaking his rhythm, Frank reached over and pounded James on the back.

Ellen sighed again. "Oh, for goodness sake, James, just take a drink."

Krissy watched in fascination as James's face went from chalk white to beet red. Finally, one solid whack from Frank sent James into the table and the offending chunk of partially chewed pot roast into the remainder of the potatoes.

"Gross!" Krissy squealed then pretended to vomit.

Grandma Naomi made angry shushing sounds as she stood up to remove the bowl from the table.

Catching a look from her mother, Krissy ended her performance and then looked over to see James's color returning to normal. He wasn't eating anymore, though only Krissy noticed.

After dinner, Krissy helped Grandma Naomi with the dishes and then went into the small, square living room to watch baseball with her dad. She didn't really like baseball, but it was the only time her usually taciturn father would talk to her. He was a loyal fan of the Cleveland Indians, despite living in south-central Ohio where everybody else rooted for the Reds.

Krissy cozied right up to Frank to listen to him explain the finer points of free agency to anyone who was listening.

After a while, Krissy noticed that James wasn't paying attention to the game or their dad. Instead, he sat staring off into space, pulling his lip out over and over again until Krissy was pretty sure he was going to pull it right off. Suddenly her "something's up" radar went off, and James became way more interesting than baseball.

The Reds were kicking Cleveland's behind in the fifth inning when the phone rang again. Krissy paid it no attention since it was most likely one of her dad's buddies calling to gloat, even though the Reds were having a terrible year. Krissy glanced over at James, whose lip was dark purple—and yet he was still pulling on it.

Ellen walked in with the phone to her ear and snapped at James and Krissy and then pointed at the stairs, a clear message that they were to go up to bed.

"No, Jen, we still haven't seen him. I don't know what to tell you. No, James doesn't know where he is either. Well of course I asked him..." The children paused on their way out of the living room to watch Ellen roll her eyes at the ceiling and shake her head. Frank grunted and then snapped his fingers for the phone as the Indians scored three runs at the end of the inning. "Listen, Jen, Frank needs the phone. How 'bout I call you if he turns up?" Ellen listened for another second. "Jen, I'm sorry...I have to go. All right...bye." Ellen let out a sigh of exasperation as she handed the phone over to Frank and then noticed that Krissy and James were still in the room. "Go on, go to bed...now!"

Krissy had her lights out, but she was far from sleepy. She stared out into the night sky and watched the stars come twinkling on, one after another. She was so engrossed with the light show that she barely heard James opening her door to creep into her room.

"Krissy?" he whispered. "Are you asleep?"

"No," she whispered back and then watched his shadow move across the room to sit at the end of her bed. "What's the matter?"

"Do you think Mason is OK?" he whispered. Even in the dark Krissy could tell his lip was swollen. It made him sound like he'd been to the dentist.

"I don't know," she answered. "I guess so. Why?"

James was quiet for a long minute. "I don't know...I guess...never mind. Go to sleep."

Krissy watched her brother creep out of the room and close the door behind him, and then she went back to staring at the sky.

Ellen

You'd think people would know better than to call during dinner, especially when it doesn't have anything to do with your own family. Ellen seethed over it during dinner and then almost pitched a fit when Jen McGee called again, disturbing their family time. Ellen had more important things to do than care about Mason McGee not coming home. You'd think people would do a better job parenting their children. She and Frank both worked and *their* kids were sitting right where they were supposed to.

And Jen sounded awfully snippy during that last phone call. Ellen was not going to stand for that. It's not her fault Frank needed the phone and it wasn't like keeping Ellen on the line was going to find her son. Some people just couldn't get their shit together.

TWO

Krissy

The next morning, a loud rapping outside woke Krissy up. A moment later she heard the screech of the screen door as whoever was outside opened it to pound on the front door. She looked over at the clock and saw that it was only 6:00 a.m. For a minute she thought it might be her dad, but he usually left earlier than six for his shift at the Honda plant. Too curious to go back to sleep, Krissy jumped out of bed and left her room to peek from the top of the stairs. Grandma Naomi, who slept in a small room off the kitchen, was just opening the door.

Krissy squatted but could only see dark-gray legs and shiny black shoes. A little lower and she could see the black holster and patches for the Clark County sheriff's department.

"Good morning, Miss Naomi. Sorry to wake you up, but I need to speak with James."

Krissy's eyes went wide as Grandma Naomi shushed the deputy into the living room. Before she could be told to, Krissy darted into James's room and shook him awake. "James," she whispered urgently. "Get up."

James rolled over and blinked at Krissy. "Whu..."

"Sheriff's here...asking for you. Get up."

James sat straight up and stared at Krissy. "Sheriff?" he whispered.

Krissy nodded. She could hear Grandma Naomi padding her way up the stairs and then tapping on her parents door.

James heard her, too, and jumped up to pull jeans over his boxer shorts. Both James and Krissy sat still as stone listening as their mother answered Grandma Naomi's knock. They could hear their mother whispering and Grandma Naomi shushing, then the sound of Ellen padding down the stairs. They strained to hear the muffled conversation going on between their mother and the deputy, and then all went quiet.

A minute later, Ellen was at James's door, her face set, her expression unreadable. She motioned for James to follow her, and after a moment's hesitation said, "You too, Krissy." The two children followed their mother down the stairs to the living room, where Deputy Martin stood waiting in the center of the small room, his thumbs stuck behind his belt buckle.

"Sorry to disturb you all so early, kids." Krissy recognized the deputy in the way children sort of know their mail carrier or the cashier at the supermarket. His was a face she'd seen before, but she'd never had an occasion to hear him speak.

Krissy turned to see her mother lift her nose and adopt the queenly air she sometimes did around people she thought of as beneath her, which to Krissy appeared to be a lot of people.

"What exactly is all this about?" Ellen sniffed. Krissy looked from her mother to the deputy, who had taken off his hat and was tucking it under his arm.

"Well, Jen McGee called us late last night, stating that her son Mason had not come home. As of this morning, he is considered missing, and Jen suggested that your boy James here might know where he is."

Ellen looked over at James as if someone might have switched her real child at birth, and then she pushed both James and Krissy toward the sofa.

Without being asked, the deputy took the chair to their right and sat down, setting his hat on the coffee table and resting his elbows on his knees.

Krissy studied Deputy Martin as he in turn studied James. She could smell the combination of soap and aftershave and saw that his hair was still wet as if he'd just showered. She suddenly felt dirty and crossed her arms over herself self-consciously. Her movement caught the deputy's eye and seemed to rouse him from his reverie.

"So, James, Mrs. McGee told us that Mason left his home early yesterday with you and several other boys."

James nodded, and Deputy Martin mirrored his response.

"Do you remember what time that was?"

James shook his head this time, and Deputy Martin again followed suit.

"Where did you go?"

James shrugged, but this time Deputy Martin just studied him.

"That's not the answer I'm looking for, son. Now, where did you go?"

James looked over at Ellen, who was standing in the doorway with her arms crossed in front of her. Krissy thought their mom looked wickedly PO'd and was pretty sure James wasn't going to admit to anything in front of her. Deputy Martin seemed to think so, too.

"Ma'am, could I trouble you for a cup of coffee?" he asked politely.

Ellen raised her eyebrow at him but nodded and then left the room.

"So, James, where was that you went again?"

"All over," James mumbled.

Deputy Martin nodded. "And how did you get there?"

"Bikes," James answered a little more loudly.

"And who was with you?" The deputy smiled encouragingly.

"Mason, Justice Guthrie, Clinton Summers, Minor Allen, and Todd Murray," James recited to the armrest. "And Krissy."

The deputy nodded again. "And where did you last see Mason McGee?"

"I didn't see him," James answered, "Krissy did."

Krissy started a little at hearing her name. She shrank as the deputy turned to look at her.

"Krissy, did you see Mason McGee yesterday?"

"Yes," Krissy answered quietly.

Deputy Marten smiled at her. "Good girl. Now where did you see Mason?"

She glanced over at James, who stared at her as if willing a thought into her head. Krissy waited a moment, but she wasn't getting any message. She turned back to the deputy.

"Crybaby Bridge," she answered.

"You mean the overpass on Pitchin Road?" he asked, and Krissy nodded. Deputy Martin's eyebrows went up and he smiled.

"Really," he said. "And what were you all doing over that way? That's pretty far from here."

To Krissy, Deputy Martin seemed so nice that she really couldn't see any reason to keep secrets. "It's where all the devil worshippers go," Krissy explained. "James and them dared me that I couldn't stand at that house over there for five minutes, and I told them that it was easy so we went and gone over there and I stood there the whole time till James threw a rock at the door and we all ran for it because the door was openin' and Mason got left behind because his bike chain came off but James didn't know because I told him that the boogeyman got Mason and then I came home." Krissy finished in a rush.

Both Deputy Martin and James stared at Krissy for a moment. Deputy Martin turned to James and asked, "And what about you, James... what did you do when Krissy told you that the boogeyman got Mason?"

James fidgeted at the question and started pulling on his lip. After a really long minute, he answered. "I told Clinton to go over and see what was takin' him so long, but he didn't see anything, so I went to go get him myself."

Deputy Martin waited a bit for James to continue, but James had clammed up.

"And what happened when you went to find Mason?"

James kept pulling on his lip and Krissy noticed that he'd cracked the skin and it was beginning to bleed. "He wasn't there," James said quietly.

Deputy Martin considered that for a moment and was about to speak when James interrupted him.

"Just his bike," James whispered, and Krissy suddenly felt goose bumps rising on her skin. Deputy Martin opened his mouth, but James spoke again. "And his shoe."

Deputy Martin and Krissy stared at James as blood traced a line from his lip down his chin. They didn't know Ellen was at the doorway until they heard her sharp intake of breath. Krissy turned to see her mother's face turn red.

For Krissy, time seemed to stop as everyone stared at each other. Then everything came rushing back as Deputy Martin jumped up, pulled his radio from his belt, and started barking into it.

Ellen turned away from the living room and Krissy heard her going back into the kitchen. She kind of hoped that her mother would come into the living room, sit between her and James, and hug them close. She wasn't sure why, but suddenly Krissy was frightened. She looked over at James and saw him watching the deputy warily. Sure enough, no sooner had Deputy Martin stepped outside, he was back inside.

"James, I'm going to need to know exactly where you saw Mason's bike."

James slowly described the spot where Krissy had last seen Mason. Deputy Martin took down notes and asked a few more questions. Krissy shook her head numbly when the deputy asked her if she had anything to add and watched him as he stepped outside with his radio squawking at him.

Krissy looked over at James to see him staring at the blood smeared all over his fingers.

"James...what happened to Mason?" she asked, her voice sounding to her as if it was coming from somewhere far away.

James looked at her as if suddenly realizing she was still there, and then he shook his head. "I don't know," he answered, his voice also coming from a distance.

Ellen

Ellen pulled her robe around her and gripped it closed just under her chin. She was absurdly conscious of how faded and threadbare it was, not anything even remotely presentable for company even if the company was just a sheriff's deputy and not anyone worth bothering over.

She could hear Naomi puttering around in the kitchen, making coffee like the queen had come to visit, and inwardly raged at the waste of perfectly good food. It wasn't likely that the deputy was going to stay very long anyway. He had a job to do, after all.

She knew the deputy was just trying to get rid of her so he could talk to the kids, and it made her bristle. They were *her* children. She had a right to know what he was going to ask them and what they were going to say. Instead of going into the kitchen, she stopped just outside the doorway to listen.

Ellen strained to hear James's monosyllabic answers and shook her head. Thank God her children were good looking. There was no way they were going to get ahead in life with their brains. Ellen blamed Frank and despaired that she'd ever married him in the first place. The man could hardly string three words together. She should have listened to her mother and married Ted Marshall instead. She'd be the wife of an insurance agent, living in her own house in Springfield instead of squatting in this tiny shack with Frank's third mother while his father pretended to be crazy.

Ellen hoped the deputy wouldn't be much longer. She had to get ready for work. She stepped back into the living room quietly, waiting for a moment to interrupt and send the deputy on his way. She didn't even know why he was here. Her kids didn't know anything.

Ellen moved closer and overheard the deputy ask, "And what happened when you went to find Mason?" She felt her face burn as rage filled her head like a thousand angry hornets. If they had anything to do with Mason going missing, she was going to kill them. This family was embarrassing enough without them losing one of their half-wit friends.

THREE

Krissy

The disappearance of Mason McGee was big news to the residents of Clark County, Ohio. At first there was a lot of talk of Mason getting lost in the woods, but Krissy privately thought that was just about the dumbest thing she had ever heard. What people called "woods" were really just small stands of trees between fields, and anybody who lived here knew you could walk an hour in just about any direction and find a Walmart. And all the kids around here knew the fields and woods better than their own bedroom floors, so the idea of Mason wandering around lost was just silly. Besides, everyone knew going to Crybaby Bridge was something all the kids did.

It was the dare that every kid made and the test of courage every kid took at some point in their lives. At first sight there wasn't really anything special about the bridge. It wasn't even that big of a bridge, more a gentle overpass that crossed the North Fork Little Miami River at one of its narrowest points. Krissy would have been surprised to find that there were several Crybaby Bridges around the state and even more in at least six other states across the country. But where other locations were thought to be haunted by the ghosts of past tragedies, Krissy's Crybaby Bridge simply had the distinction of being frequented by more human haunts in the form of various disenfranchised teens who enjoyed their nonconformist lifestyle by wearing a uniform of black clothing, white faces, and black lipstick. During their time at the local high school, they frequented the bridge, not because of its reputation but because of its location away from the usual path of the sheriff's patrol car.

The bridge itself wasn't called anything until an aspiring art student used a dead tree near the bridge as the setting for an art installation of old baby dolls. The goth kids liked it so much they made it their favorite spot to smoke and complain about their parents. As the goth kids graduated and moved on to bigger, or lesser, things, the baby dolls remained, and rumor that the dead tree was a site for sacrifices to Satan grew into legend.

By noon the next day, though, the sheriff's department had recruited just about everyone in the county to help in the search for Mason McGee.

Krissy sat at the kitchen window and stared out into the distance as a line of grown-ups wearing Day-Glo orange vests made their way slowly across Mr. Harper's hay field. Every so often one would swat out at a fluttering cicada as it was knocked off its grass stalk. At one point, one of the volunteers stopped and flapped around, disturbing a whole bunch of cicadas until the guy next to him reached over and pulled a cicada out of his shirt. Another line of volunteers moved through the corn, though they were less visible. Only the uneven movement of the corn and the occasional splash of an orange vest gave away their location.

"What are they looking for?" Krissy asked Grandma Naomi as she washed their lunch dishes. Grandma Naomi shushed something that sounded an awful lot like "body," which came so darn close to a deeply hidden fear that Krissy didn't ask for clarification. Instead, she glanced at James, who was picking at the last of his sandwich with a horrible grimace on his face. Krissy realized that he'd heard the same thing. James stared at Grandma Naomi for a moment, his face twisted and pinched, and then turned and looked out the window.

As they watched the volunteers inch along like an orange caterpillar leaving its trail in the newly trampled hay, their mother walked in with a huff and a snap at Grandma Naomi.

"Did you move my heels, Naomi?" Ellen barked. "I am extremely late for work and I need them now." Grandma Naomi threw her dishtowel aside and left the room as Ellen poured coffee into her travel mug. "I can't believe they're keeping me from leaving," she snapped. "What could I possibly do to help them? Nothing, that's what." She sighed elaborately as she stirred sugar into her coffee and looked to see what Krissy and James were staring at. "Well, that's just great," she groused. "I hope they didn't tramp through our lawn. They'll kill the grass."

Krissy turned and frowned at her mother, who was staring at the volunteers with her lips clenched into the thinnest of lines. Why on earth would her mother think those people needed to come through their yard? Their grass was about as long as a minute and the yard was so small it only took three trips around the house with the lawn mower and the gardening was done.

"Ugh, finally," Ellen grunted as Grandma Naomi walked in carrying her black heels. "If they ask, tell them I just couldn't stay any longer," she said sharply as she stepped into her heels, and with her coffee in hand, she stalked out the door without so much as a good-bye to anyone.

Krissy stared wistfully after her mother then looked over at James, who was still watching the volunteers.

"James," Krissy asked quietly, "why do they keep asking about Mason's bike?"

James shrugged without looking away from the window. "Probably because of the chain."

Krissy watched as James tenderly pinched his lower lip, breaking the scab. "What about it?" she asked.

James ignored her for a moment as if he didn't know what she meant. "What about what?" he asked finally.

"The chain," she persisted.

James glanced at Krissy and then returned his gaze to the slowly retreating line of orange vests. He was quiet for a really long time. Krissy watched as he pulled his hand away from his lip and stared at the blood on his fingers. Then he looked at her and mumbled, "It was fixed."

Krissy spent the rest of the day in her room watching the constant movement of sheriff's deputies and volunteers as they crisscrossed the landscape. She was surprised to see Mr. Harper come out and help in the search of his hay field. She figured he'd be out waving his shotgun around at the sight of all his fine hay being trampled, but he didn't seem to mind. In fact, he even sent his nephew, Zach, to check on all the out-buildings. Krissy didn't mind watching Zach, his being so handsome and all. She knew lots of older girls who went all dreamy over Zach, though he didn't seem to like any of them. Krissy wondered if maybe he was waiting for her to grow up so they could run off together and get married.

She was so lost in her daydreaming that she hardly noticed James when he pushed his bike around the corner of the house. Happy to be able to remind him that they weren't supposed to go anywhere, Krissy pressed her face against the screen.

"James!" she called out. "You're not supposed to be going anywhere!"

James turned and scowled at her and put his finger to his lips. Krissy climbed down off her bed and flew down the stairs. James was waiting for her at the bottom of the front walk.

"Where are you going?" she whispered so loudly the cashiers at Walmart most likely turned to see who was standing behind them.

"Shut up, Krissy!" James hissed. "You're gonna bring Naomi out here!"

Krissy shook her head. "She's sleeping in front of the TV."

James looked past her as if he didn't believe her. "Still, you're gonna have to be quiet."

"Where are you going?" Krissy asked again, more quietly.

James threw his leg over his bike and sat down. "Me and the guys are goin' to look for Mason."

Krissy looked at him blankly for a moment. "Well, what good's that gonna do when everyone's lookin' for him? If he was gonna be found... well, they woulda found him by now," she said in a moment of unintentional yet chilling clarity.

James looked exactly like their mother as he pressed his lips together in a scowl. "They're lookin' for him in the wrong places. They're not gonna know all the places we go to."

"Who's going with you?" Krissy asked, wanting to stall him and maybe stall that queasy knotted feeling in the pit of her stomach.

"Justice, Minor, and Todd." James looked impatient.

"Why can't you just tell that Deputy Martin where to look?"

James shook his head at Krissy as if she were impossibly stupid. "If I tell them everywhere we go then we'll get in trouble. If we find Mason, then they won't care where it was."

Krissy stared at her brother while trying to think of another question. The need to keep him from going was gnawing at her insides so badly she almost doubled over. "Why isn't Clinton going with you?" she asked lamely.

"His mom's keeping him home." James had had enough of the Q & A. He turned his bike toward the drive.

"James," Krissy called out with so much panic in her voice her brother actually stopped and looked back at her. "Don't go."

James looked at her with the grimmest expression she'd ever seen on her brother's face. For that long moment, he looked like a grown-up. "Cover for me, OK?" He pedaled off in a cloud of dust.

Krissy went back into the house and spent the rest of the afternoon pacing the kitchen. She didn't dare wake Grandma Naomi lest she tell on James when their parents got home. Instead, she went back and forth across the worn vinyl floor, one eye always out the window. From her bedroom window, she had seen James meet up with his friends at the end of the driveway and ride off toward the bridge.

For a little while she felt like they were going to turn around and come right back, but as the light began to fade, Krissy felt like maybe she should have told on him. Then, just as the light took on that weird green that made all the colors of the landscape deepen, she saw James slowly turn into their driveway. He was covered in dirt and pedaling slowly as if it hurt him to move.

Krissy tiptoed quietly down the steps so as not to waken Grandma Naomi, who was now snoring in front of the six o'clock news. She made it out the door in time to see James slide off his bike seat. She waited as he pushed his bike a couple of feet farther onto the front walk, too tired to go any farther, and he dropped it onto the ground with a clang that woke Grandma Naomi. James sat down hard on the step where Krissy stood. Krissy kept quiet until Grandma Naomi peeked her head out at them and turned away. When they were sure she was heading toward the kitchen, they began to whisper. "Well?" she asked.

James just shook his head. "Nothing. We didn't find nothing."

"Where did you go?"

"Everywhere. We went from Shawnee to Yellow Springs and then up to the highway and back."

Krissy stared at her brother. "That must be like...thirty miles!" Krissy didn't really know how far it was, but thirty miles sounded far.

James nodded. "Something like that."

"Didn't anyone see you?"

"No, not anyone important." James slowly lifted his hand and rubbed his face.

Krissy glanced down the driveway. "Where are the others?"

James yawned. "Gone home...Justice took a fall so he left first."

Krissy felt sorry for Justice Guthrie. He was just about the nicest boy ever who lived near the elementary school with his grandmother. "Is he all right?"

James nodded. "He just lost some skin on his hand."

Both fell silent for the moment. As James rested, Krissy's mind churned doubts and suspicions. One in particular kept jumping out at her, but she was afraid to tell James in case he laughed at her or called her stupid.

"James?" she began, despite herself.

"Hmm," he grunted in answer, his eyes still closed.

"Who lives in the house at Crybaby Bridge?"

James shrugged in answer and ventured, "Why?"

Krissy stared at James without seeing him, all the while flicking her lower lip with a nervous "plop."

James opened his eyes and looked at his sister. "Why?" he asked again.

Krissy let go of her lip and, tucking her hands under her folded arms, looked at James carefully. "Maybe that's where Mason is," she answered. "Maybe whoever lives there took him."

James stared at his sister for a good long moment and then shook his head. "Naw, I don't think he's there."

"Why not?"

"'Cause nobody lives there," he yawned.

"Yuh-huh," Krissy insisted. "When you hit the door with that rock, it started opening."

James shook his head again. "No it didn't, Krissy. You just got scared and ran."

This time it was Krissy's turn to shake her head. "I didn't run when you hit the door...I ran when it started to open."

"I still don't think so. No one lives there like it's their house. I don't think it even is a house. Besides, no one can get in with that fence all the way around it," James argued.

"Then why is it there?" Krissy argued back.

"What...the fence?" James looked confused.

"No...the house. If no one is supposed to live there, then why is there a house at Crybaby Bridge?"

James didn't have an answer for that. "It doesn't matter anyway. There's all kinds of run-down shacks around here that are easier to get to. We already found a couple that we're gonna go back and check out."

"I don't think so," Krissy said slowly.

"You don't think so what?" James asked, though she could tell he didn't really care.

"I don't think it doesn't matter." A thought kept churning in her head, but she didn't know how to say it aloud so that it would make sense.

"Why would it matter?" James asked through a huge yawn.

"Because it's the closest place to where Mason disappeared," she answered. She knew it made sense and she couldn't understand why she was the only one who thought so.

That evening, sure that their mother wouldn't notice, Krissy continued to shoot pointed looks at James, who did his best to ignore her. The idea that Mason was stuck in that house made perfect sense to her. Why couldn't her brother see it?

Krissy gave up on James and finished her dinner in a sulk. Their mother noticed, though, and sent Krissy upstairs without dessert. James followed shortly, much to his sister's surprise. She was even more surprised when he stepped into her room and closed the door behind him.

"I didn't mean that looking was a bad idea. We already went and looked at the house," he said as he sat at the end of her bed. Krissy watched him silently, almost afraid of what he was going to say. "There isn't any way to get in or out of that fence." James yawned. "There's no gate or holes or nothing."

"Did you check inside?" Krissy asked.

"You can see the whole yard through the fence," he began.

"Not the yard," Krissy interrupted, "the house."

James sighed. "I told you, there's no way to get through that fence. How are we gonna look in the house if we can't even get through the fence?"

It was Krissy's turn to be without an answer, so she let the matter drop. James looked totally beat and got up to leave. "James?" she asked as he opened her door. James looked at her with weary eyes.

"Yeah?"

Krissy paused for a moment and then sighed. "Never mind."

James shook his head and let himself out of the room.

Ellen

Ellen hung up the phone, tired and annoyed. Mothers across the county were calling each other to gossip about the disappearance of Mason McGee. Ellen was so tired of talking about a kid she hardly knew that she began cutting the conversations short and hanging up, especially when the women started talking about setting up a casserole calendar for his mother, Jen. Ellen wasn't about to start cooking for another family just because their kid got lost somewhere. Jesus Christ, half these kids were so stupid they couldn't find their assholes with a map. If Naomi wanted to make something that was fine, but Ellen would have to make sure she didn't use their food. If Naomi thought she was going to spend a penny of Ellen's hard-earned pay on someone else, Ellen would be happy to set her straight.

FOUR

Krissy

This time Krissy was a little bit awake when she heard the knock on the door, as if she already knew something was wrong. The world just didn't feel right and Krissy hoped deep down inside that it wasn't too bad.

Still in that knowing way, Krissy didn't bother to get out of bed to see who it was. She knew it was Deputy Martin back to talk to James, and as much as she wanted it to be anything else, she felt in her heart that Justice was gone.

As the rest of the house awoke with noises of confusion and irritation, Krissy lay quietly under her quilt and stared blankly at the ceiling as if this next terrible drama was being projected there. She listened keenly as the deputy again asked to speak with James, then Grandma Naomi's footsteps on the stairs. The sound of the knock on her parents' door and the creak as it opened. The sigh her mother made when her children were being impossibly inconvenient, then the creak of James's door.

This time it seemed the deputy only wanted to speak to James, since no one came in to fetch her.

When she was sure everyone was downstairs, Krissy crawled out of bed and crept to her door, which she opened with as little noise as possible.

The sound of voices downstairs spurred her forward to the top of the stairs, where she paused before carefully creeping halfway down to where she could just see into the front half of the living room.

This time Deputy Martin wasn't interested in being James's friend. "...and I need to know where you boys went yesterday and why."

Krissy couldn't hear James's mumbled answer, but through the screen door she caught sight of three sheriff's cars jammed into her driveway and two deputies leaning against them with their hands resting on the butts of their guns. They were talking to each other and they looked pissed. Krissy suddenly felt sick to her stomach. James was in huge trouble if they thought they might have to shoot him. She watched as they looked all around in case James might be sneaking up on them in his underwear. As soon as she realized that they could probably see her through the screen door, Krissy had a sudden and desperate urge to pee. It became so intense that her bladder began to cramp. Unable to hold it any longer, Krissy darted up the stairs. When she was done, she crept back to the top of the steps. She leaned against the railing to listen but could only make out a few words. After a few minutes she gave up and went down into the kitchen, where she found Grandma Naomi pouring several cups of coffee. Without being told, Krissy got out a box of cookies, poured them on a plate, and placed it on the tray next to Grandma Naomi's coffee. Grandma Naomi turned and looked at Krissy for a long moment and then began to talk.

Krissy wanted to pretend to not understand, but she knew better. She understood everything Grandma Naomi was asking her even if she didn't know the answers. She even understood why Grandma Naomi was so upset. Justice Guthrie was missing now and his grandmother was Grandma Naomi's best friend.

Krissy was happy that Grandma Naomi couldn't talk or she'd be yelling right now, and that would surely bring in the deputy. Instead of answering, Krissy just stood in the middle of the kitchen shaking her head. Grandma Naomi had figured out that James and his friends had gone off yesterday, and she was hopping mad that they had thought to take Justice with them as if there was any better reason to take anyone else.

Eventually Grandma Naomi ran out of steam and gave up on Krissy. With a sour look, she picked up the tray and carried it out of the kitchen.

When Krissy was sure she was alone, she fell into her chair at the kitchen table with a sigh and looked around longingly for her breakfast.

It wasn't until much later that Grandma Naomi got around to feeding anybody, and even then it was only the deputies. Then, as soon as she could make herself understood, Grandma Naomi got one of them to drive her over to the Guthrie house where she stayed for the rest of the day.

Krissy and, eventually, James had to make do with cold cereal and toast since their mother drove off just after the deputies, leaving her children to look after themselves.

Krissy watched her mother speed down the driveway in a cloud of dust and felt suddenly afraid. She turned to her brother.

"James?"

"Hmmphf," he answered through a mouthful of cereal.

"What if *he* comes here?" she asked quietly as if someone might be listening.

James didn't bother to look up from his bowl but asked, "He who?"

"The man who took Mason and Justice." She lowered her voice even more. "What if he comes here?"

That brought James up short and he stared at his sister with a mouth full of cereal. Krissy watched as it took a long time for him to swallow. Then he shook his head slowly. "No one's coming here, Kris." James tried to sound calm, but Krissy could tell she had rattled him.

She wanted to ask how he could know that, but she really didn't want to know the answer.

With no one to watch them, Krissy and James stayed close to home, never venturing further than the fence on the other side of the drive-way. At lunchtime, Krissy made an attempt at macaroni and cheese. She'd earned a Brownie patch for cooking, though Krissy suspected it was more for effort than anything else. At any rate, with some tuna mixed in and a little red pepper sauce on top, it was at least edible. After lunch, Krissy made no-bake cookie dough that she and James ate right out of the bowl on the front steps.

They were fighting over the last spoonful when a crunch on the drive startled them into silence. They had been so intent on their argument that they didn't notice Mr. Harper's nephew, Zach, walking up the drive.

Up close he was even better looking than Krissy had thought, with his black hair and eyes so dark they looked black as well. She had no idea how old he was...twenty, thirty, forty. Well, probably not forty. Then he would be too old for her when she would finally be old enough to date. His handsome features were twisted into an expression of concern.

"Hey," he called out, even though both Krissy and James were staring at him. "You guys here alone?"

"Yea...ugh," Krissy began, but James shoved the bowl into her so hard he almost knocked her off the step.

"No, our dad's inside," James interrupted.

Zach looked at the house and cocked his head a little. "Really? I don't hear anything."

Krissy sat very still and wondered why James was lying. Zach only needed to look at the empty carport to see no one was home.

"He's sleeping," James lied some more. "He works nights."

Zach stared at James and then looked at Krissy. "I thought I saw your dad leaving early this morning. Are you sure you're not alone?"

Krissy shook her head as James answered. "He came back when the sheriff's deputies came over. They're coming back, too."

Zach's smile was kind. "I hope so. I'd hate to see anything happen to you two." He looked off across the cornfields and sighed. "Those were two good boys who disappeared. It'd be a shame to lose you, too."

James seemed to consider this and softened up a little. "Yeah, well, we're not planning on disappearing." Krissy shook her head as if to confirm this.

Zach looked at her intently and Krissy's stomach did flip-flops. "If you need anything, let me know." He nodded over to Mr. Harper's farm. "I asked my uncle not to fuss if you guys needed to cut through the field for help."

James nodded. "Thanks."

Zach turned to go. "Tell your dad I said hi."

When he was out of earshot, Krissy whispered, "Why did you tell him dad was home?"

James shrugged. "I don't know. I just didn't feel like him knowing we were home alone."

"Why not? He could have helped us," Krissy insisted.

"Helped us how?" James looked at her with an expression that was both hopeful and hopeless.

Krissy panicked. She'd never seen her brother look like that. "I don't know, but it's better than being alone, right?"

James scowled and shrugged. "Maybe."

That evening, after dinner, Krissy sat close to her father as he watched the news. It was way past her bedtime, but her dad hadn't said anything yet, and her mother wasn't around to remind her, having left to pick up Grandma Naomi from the Guthrie house.

James was about to head up to bed when a story about the cicadas ended and the report about Mason and Justice began. Krissy didn't realize what they were talking about until the report was almost done.

"...in an exclusive interview with former sheriff Richard Brown. Channel seven news reporter Mindy Newton investigated the disappearance of four boys in 2004. Scott Davis, Kirk Harper, Tony Douglas, and Brian Tucker were all from Clark County, the same community now facing the tragic disappearance of two more boys this past week."

Krissy looked from the television to her father, who sat staring at the plastic smiles of the news anchors. Out of the corner of her eye she could see James still staring at the television, his expression as grim as her father's. "Daddy?" she ventured quietly so as not to remind him she wasn't supposed to be there.

"Hmm," he grunted.

"Was Kirk Harper related to Mr. Harper?"

Krissy shrank a bit as James and her father both turned to look at her as if surprised to see her still there. She worried for a moment that her father would send her to bed rather than answer. Then he yawned.

"Kirk was Mr. Harper's younger son," her father answered tiredly. "He was about twelve or thirteen when he disappeared. Scott and Tony were his best friends. Brian Tucker was one of my church youth."

"Is that why Mr. Harper was so nice about all those people walking through his fields?"

"Probably." Her dad nodded and then rubbed his hand across his face. When he was done he looked melted, like a candle left in the sun. "Tom and Patty Harper only had Kirk and Jeremy. He was torn up to lose a child like that...it half broke Patty's heart."

"What happened to their other son?" Krissy asked, hoping her dad wouldn't notice the time.

"Jeremy went to stay with his grandparents just in case."

"Is that why Zach lives at the farm now, to help him?" Krissy ventured.

"No." Her dad shook his head. "Zach moved in about a year before it all happened. He's been there the whole time. Now you two need to go to bed before your mother gets back and we all catch hell." He leaned over and gave Krissy a rare kiss on the forehead, then shooed her and James toward the stairs. Krissy knew he meant business when he turned the television off.

James seemed lost in thought as they made their way up to their rooms. His quiet made Krissy uncomfortable and nervous. She wanted to ask him what he was thinking, but he went into his room without saying a word. He didn't even look at her as he closed the door behind him.

Krissy went into her room and fell into bed, grateful that cicadas didn't sing at night.

Ellen

When Ellen got up the next morning it was to find a note from Frank saying he'd taken Naomi back to the Guthrie woman's house. Ellen shook her head in disgust. What possible reason could Naomi have for going back over there?

She fumed as she took a quick shower and got dressed. Even though it was her day off, the last thing she wanted to do was sit around while Krissy and James either slept the day away or stared at the television like half-wits. At least the mall had air conditioning.

Ellen didn't bother to leave a note. Those kids weren't likely to wake up until the afternoon anyway. She'd be home long before then.

FIVE

Krissy

The next morning, Krissy slept through breakfast. By the time she woke up, bleary-eyed and headachy, it was after ten o'clock, and the house was silent but for the metallic buzz of the millions of cicadas that had made Mr. Harper's fields and border trees their home.

Instead of getting out of bed, Krissy lay staring out her window at the bright blue sky. Whatever time it was, it was already hot, and the thought of spending another day at home made her grumpy.

When she couldn't take the heat any longer, Krissy rolled out of bed and melted into the bathroom to stand under a cold shower. When she was good and cold, she stepped out and pulled a comb through her long, brown hair and then walked back into her bedroom to put on some clothes.

Downstairs, she found James at the kitchen table with his Nintendo, but instead of playing Pokémon, he was staring out the kitchen window.

"Where's Grandma Naomi?" Krissy asked as she pulled down a box of cereal and a bowl.

It took a while for James to realize she was there. "Oh, um, back at Justice's house."

Krissy sat across from her brother and poured milk over her cereal but didn't eat. A twisted knot was beginning to form in the pit of her stomach, leaving no room for food. She stared into the bowl, her spoon clenched in her fist.

Krissy didn't want to let James know it, but she was really, really afraid. More than anything she wished her mother, or at least Grandma Naomi, was home to watch over them. She looked over at her brother and noticed that the back door was closed and locked when it was usually left wide open in case a breeze wanted to come and visit through the screen door. She didn't have to check to know that the front door was probably locked as well. When Krissy glanced back at James, she realized that he too was scared.

"What are we going to do?" she asked with a quiver in her voice.

James finally looked at her as if she were actually there. "About what?"

"About being by ourselves."

James shook his head and looked away. Krissy didn't like that he didn't have an answer.

With the house to themselves, Krissy and James spent the majority of the day in front of the television. She wasn't sure, but Krissy thought she might have slept for a while, and she was sure that neither of them ate any lunch.

At six o'clock, their mother walked through the door. She stopped at the stairs and stared down the hall to the kitchen.

"Ugh!" she said in disgust and turned and walked back out the front door.

Krissy hungrily watched her mother's retreating back, wishing for a hug or kiss, or anything. Instead she heard the car door slam and the engine start. Either their mother was going to get something for dinner, was picking up Grandma Naomi, or was running away forever. Krissy hoped that if her mother ran away forever she'd take them with her, but in the darkest place of her heart, she knew they'd be left behind.

Krissy's eyes welled with tears as James snored lightly beside her. Almost worse than her mother's angry exit was the fact that in her haste to leave, she'd left the front door wide open. Krissy stared as the screen door tapped softly against the door frame where it had been left unlatched. Too afraid to pull it closed and expose herself, she gently tapped James awake.

"Whu? Huh?" he stammered as he pushed himself upright on the couch. "What?"

"The door," Krissy whispered. "Mom left the door open."

"Door?" Still bleary, James looked over at the door, then jumped up and ran over to slam it closed so fast that Krissy let out a little squeak of surprise. "Where did Mom go?" James asked as he quickly returned to the couch.

Krissy shrugged. "She walked in and then made an angry sound and left."

James looked at her for a moment, then turned to stare at the door.

Ellen

Un-freaking-believable, Ellen raged as she sped down the driveway. When Frank dropped Naomi off at the Guthrie house, he must have figured Ellen would make dinner...like she even had the time after being away the whole day.

She barely stopped at the end of the driveway, where a patrol car had parked. Out of the corner of her eye she spotted the deputy inside giving her a half-hearted wave, which only made her angrier. Ellen put her nose up and turned away, then pulled onto the road, more sedately so as not to give the idiot behind her a reason to pull her over.

This is just so damn typical, she said to herself. Frank had no respect for her and how busy she was. He always assumed she had plenty of time to take care of the damn kids just because he worked twelve-hour shifts doing nothing but looking at shit that had already been made. Ridiculous.

And if Frank though she was going to go out of her way to schlep Naomi back and forth, he had another thing coming. She had better things to do.

She was so angry she almost drove right past the KFC. Ellen pulled in at the last minute, cutting off a minivan trying to get out. Luckily the driver didn't honk, or Ellen would have gone right over the edge.

Ellen stomped into the restaurant and barked her order to the loser standing behind the register, then tapped the counter impatiently while they took forever to get her food.

Minutes that felt like hours later, with food in hand, Ellen made her way home and dropped it on the table, ignoring the look on her children's faces. Since the table wasn't going to set itself, she grabbed plates and napkins and dropped them next to the bag.

"Well, come on," she barked, then watched as Krissy and James jumped up and hurried to the table. "You can get your own drinks," she continued, less loudly but no less angry. "I need to change." Ellen stalked away from the table and went upstairs. The smell of the food was making her sick and she had some phone calls to make.

SIX

Krissy

When their mother returned, it was to find them both still on the couch in the now-dark living room. Krissy and James had been too scared to get up to turn on the light, though neither would admit to it.

Instead of Grandma Naomi, Ellen had brought KFC for dinner. With another angry sound, she dropped it on the dinner table and then stomped into the kitchen. A moment later she returned with plates and napkins.

"Well, come on," she barked. Krissy and James jumped up and hurried to the table. "You can get your own drinks," she continued, less loudly but no less angry. "I need to change."

Krissy watched her mother's retreating back and wished with all her heart for a hug, a kiss hello, or even a pat on the head. James didn't seem to need anything from their mother anymore. Instead, he stared at the food as if it might be laced with poison.

"What would you like to drink?" she asked quietly. James shook his head sadly, still staring at their dinner.

Later that evening, they sat with their father and watched yet another baseball game while their mother spent the majority of the evening on the phone.

"Well, I heard the kidnapper is targeting good-looking children," she gossiped, staring off into space. "Mason was a nice-looking boy and Justice was downright handsome. Oh, no, I'm sure *you* needn't be worried, Clinton looks too much like his father did. Obviously I'm concerned...my children look like me, of course they're at risk."

Krissy looked over at James, who sat on the other side of their father. She saw that he too had been listening. James glanced over at her and then stood up and stomped out of the room. Krissy and her father listened as James stomped all the way up the stairs and into his bedroom. Then her father turned to her.

"You go up too, Krissy," he said quietly. "Make sure your brother is OK."

Krissy nodded and did as she was told. As she ascended the steps, she felt her chest grow tight and her eyes burn hot and wet. Instead of James's room, Krissy took a detour to the bathroom and closed the door behind her. She sat down on the toilet seat and pulled her knees up to her chin. Her tears fell quietly as she rocked back and forth, trying to calm herself.

When she was finally spent, Krissy stood and washed her face without looking at herself in the mirror. Then she opened the door. She wasn't sure how long she had been in there, but she could hear her mother still on the phone and James's bedroom light shone from under his door. Krissy knocked more quietly than she intended. "James?"

From the other side of the door she heard James answer but couldn't understand him. She opened the door and peered around it to see her brother on his bed with his knees pulled up, his eyes red like he'd just been crying. Krissy carefully closed the door behind her and crept to the end of his bed and sat.

"Are you OK?" she whispered.

James angrily scrubbed at his eyes. "I'm fine," he snapped. His expression turned bleak. "I don't know what to do. It's my fault that Justice is missing now too. And I can't leave you here alone to go look for him."

Krissy was suddenly terrified that he would do just that. "The police and all the volunteers will look for him now. It's not like when it was just Mason and people thought he was playing around. The sheriffs know it's for real," she said in a rush.

James gave her the kindest look she'd ever seen on his face directed toward her. "Don't worry, Kris. I'm not going to go unless Grandma Naomi is here. And if I have to leave, I'll take you with me."

Krissy's smile was weak and full of tears but genuine.

James's expression turned thoughtful. "Can you still ride your bike?"

Krissy nodded. "Why?"

"Clinton has a map of the whole county. We're going to go to the library tomorrow to find out about those other kids that went missing. You're gonna have to come with."

Krissy went ice cold at the thought of leaving the safety of their little house, but she nodded.

45

Ellen

Ellen sat fuming. She tried her mother's number a hundred times already and it kept going to voicemail. If she had her phone unplugged, Ellen was going to kill her. Frank came in while she was still dialing and got ready for bed. Ellen glared at his back and then sat stunned when he crawled into bed and went to sleep without saying a single word to her.

SEVEN

Krissy

The next morning, Krissy and James came downstairs to find their dad still home and waiting for them in the kitchen. Their mother was in the process of filling her travel mug with coffee. She was in midrant about Grandma Naomi when they walked in and sat at the table.

"I don't know what she's thinking, staying at the Guthrie's when she needs to be here watching her grandchildren."

"They're not her grandchildren," Frank said quietly.

"...and when we put a roof over her head and food in her mouth..."

"It's her house," he replied, but their mom wasn't listening.

"...I can't continue to rearrange my schedule like this. I have to work to put food in our own mouths..."

"You could quit today if you wanted to."

Krissy watched her dad's face. Even though it was quiet, her father's voice had that almost-angry sound to it.

47

Ellen turned on her husband. "Quit? How am I supposed to quit? We have a lifestyle to maintain and it's not going to happen on one income."

Krissy looked over at her mother. She was dressed in an ill-fitting suit she'd bought off the clearance rack at Dress Barn, even though most of her coworkers wore either scrubs or jeans to work. Krissy knew her shoes were from Payless because she got them for half off when she bought Krissy's gym shoes for school, and her purse was a Coach bag she'd bought at a purse party. Krissy's dad had made a big deal over that purse until her mom admitted it was fake. It was only a few months old and its seams were already coming undone. Krissy stared at her mother and wondered what lifestyle meant.

"You'd better go," her father said quietly.

Krissy didn't expect a kiss and didn't get one when her mother grabbed her things and left.

Frank rubbed his face as if trying to get the tired off of it and then looked at James, who had been staring at a burn spot in their table the whole time.

"I'm going to go and see if I can't get Naomi to come back and stay with you kids. Even if she has to bring Lynne Guthrie with her, at least you won't be alone," he said, then turned and pulled a plastic store bag off the shelf behind him. "Until then I want you to stay home and keep the doors locked." He set the bag on the table and rested his hand on top of it. "But if you can't stay home, I want you to take your sister with you. Under no circumstances do you leave her alone. And I want you to take these with you and keep them on you wherever you go."

Frank opened the bag and pulled out two cell phones. They looked like simplified versions of their dad's phone. Krissy was secretly thrilled when her father pushed a purple one toward her. Nobody in her class had their own cell phone yet. Well, except for one girl, Paige, who had her dad's old iPhone. Krissy's wasn't sure it even worked.

James and Krissy turned the phones on and started pushing buttons. Their dad had already programmed phone numbers in so they could call him or their mother in case something happened.

"These are for emergencies only," Frank warned, but Krissy could see him smiling a little. "You can call, text, play music, and I even put a couple of games on them. You can't go online with them, though, and you have to be careful with the emergency button. I want you to text me when you get up and if you leave the house. If you leave you have to tell me where you're going. If I text you, I want you to text me back right away. If you don't then I'm going to call the sheriff."

"This is cool," James whispered, his eyes glued to his new phone. "Thanks, Dad."

Frank smiled. "You're welcome. Now watch the battery. The more you do, the more you drain the battery. Make sure you plug your phone into the charger every night." Frank watched his children as they intuitively navigated the phone's features with the expertise of children born into the technological age. "Remember, kids, these phones aren't toys. They're to be used in case of an emergency. In case something...happens."

Krissy and James looked at their father and nodded soberly. Then in an uncharacteristic gesture, Frank stood and stepped to the other side of the table then knelt to pull his children into his arms. Krissy melted into her father right away. James stiffened at first but then relaxed and let his father hold him.

"I know things aren't easy for you two...and I don't say it every day... but I want you to know how much I love you."

Tears came to Krissy's eyes. She wrapped her arms around her father and brother and held on tight. Frank tightened his hold on his children then let them go to look at them. James's eyes were red. He surreptitiously wiped them with the back of his hand. Frank looked closely at his son. "I want you to take care of your sister. Understand? No ditching her." James nodded as Frank turned to Krissy. "And I don't want you arguing with your brother or pestering him. You're a team and you have to take care of each other. OK?" Krissy nodded.

Frank gave his children another hug and stood. "I have to go to work now. Remember what I said about those phones. I'll try to bring Naomi home tonight." He gave them each a kiss on the head and left out the back door.

Krissy got up and got them milk and cereal while James continued to navigate the features on his phone. She set a bowl in front of him and sat down and filled her bowl.

"Are we still going to the library?" she asked.

James shook his head. "Minor's mom stayed home and she won't let him leave, and Clinton said he's supposed to go to his grandma's until they find Justice and Mason."

Ellen

By the time she got to the hospital, Ellen had a splitting headache. She was late enough that all of the good parking spots were gone, which put her in an even worse mood. She was fuming as she made her way through the staff entrance and into the suite of offices, ignoring everyone she passed who may or may not have said hello. Ellen dumped her handbag on her desk and sat down heavily. She knew she was needed out in the patient intake area, but she needed to calm down and get herself together first. It wouldn't be professional to walk out there angry and disheveled.

Ellen pulled a compact from her purse and checked her makeup and hair. To her surprise she looked exactly as she did ten minutes ago in her bathroom mirror. She put her compact away, stowed her purse in the desk, and went out.

There were only a few patients waiting when Ellen took a seat at her cubicle in the admitting section of the outpatient care unit. Ellen fired up her computer and then stepped over to check the sign-in sheet. Everyone was assigned to another cubicle, so Ellen went back to her computer to check for messages.

"You're late again, Ellen," she heard behind her. Ellen turned to see Rick, the unit administrative manager, standing behind her. She couldn't stand Rick and his weird mustache and effeminate mannerisms. He was dumb, too. Ellen knew she could do his entire job in half the time it took him to figure out how to tie his shoes, and she was doing two jobs already.

"The police were at my house again," she said, trying for a more modest tone even though she wanted to scream at him. "Another one of my son's friends went missing and they are very concerned about his well-being. This has been very hard for my family."

Rick frowned at her. "Isn't it harder on the families whose kids are missing?" he asked, and Ellen seethed. She knew he didn't like her and wanted to get her fired but couldn't. A few months ago, she had found a pile of reports that he hadn't filed and hid them until the hospital administration was screaming. When they were good and mad at Rick, Ellen conveniently found them and offered to clean up the backlog. Rick had quietly accused her of taking the files, but since he couldn't prove it, there wasn't anything he could do.

Ellen widened her eyes at him. "How can you even say that? You have no idea what we've been through. My son is terrified."

"Then shouldn't you be home with him? Since he's so terrified, and all," Rick said, his tone veering dangerously in the sarcasm zone as far as Ellen was concerned. Out of the corner of her eye she could see one of her coworkers, Missy, staring at her.

"I can't just take time off, Rick," Ellen answered, her voice going up a register. "I have responsibilities here and I can't believe you're attacking me like this. Children are *missing*."

Ellen was about to continue when one of the patients in the waiting area stood and shouted at them.

"Stop it...just stop...," she yelled, then ran out the door crying.

Ellen was stunned and immediately offended. "Who does she think she is, yelling at me like that?"

"That was Mary Davis," Missy said quietly. "Her son Scott was one of the boys who went missing before."

Ellen shook her head in disgust. "That was *ten years ago*. My son is in danger *now*."

EIGHT

Krissy

While their mother argued her case for sympathy, Krissy and James sat in Krissy's window and watched another long line of volunteers creep up the far hill where Mr. Harper's corn was high enough to hide two middle school boys. They could also see Zach and two of the sheriff's deputies searching through all of the barns and outbuildings of the Harper's farm, then make their way to the far side of the farm where a set of barns that had originally belonged to Grandpa Nate still stood. The breeze sent ripples through the stalks. To Krissy, when the wind blew it sounded like whispers. The corn shared secrets with itself that it wouldn't share with anyone else.

"Why are they doing that?" Krissy asked, nodding at the barn closest to their house.

James turned away from the volunteers in time to see Zach sliding the door closed and locking it. "They're looking in everyone's barn. They were at Minor's house yesterday and made him open every building on the farm...even the tool shed. Minor said they told his mom they were checking in case Justice and Mason ran away and were hiding somewhere."

Krissy shook her head. "Justice would never leave his grandma alone. Did she tell them that?"

James gave his sister a look. "Why would she know that?" he asked, his tone scornful. "Parents don't know things like that."

Krissy kept silent. She knew James was right. There were a ton of things parents didn't know about their kids.

By noon, the volunteers had finished the Harper's farm and had moved into the woods that marked the end of the Harper's property and the beginning of the farm on the other side. Krissy wondered if they were going to search by the bridge, but her thought was interrupted by the rumbling of her belly. She went downstairs to make peanut butter and jelly sandwiches. She didn't hear the car drive up until it was already at the house. James bounded down the stairs and opened the front door before the deputy could knock. This time it was a different deputy and Krissy was pretty sure it was the one who came to the schools to talk about safety. They announced him as Deputy Safety, but Krissy knew his real last name was Howell.

"Are either of your parents home?" he asked, peering in through the screen door.

James shook his head. "They're at work."

The deputy frowned. "What about your grandma? Where is she?"

Since it was a deputy, James chose not to lie. "She's at the Guthrie's."

"Who's here with you?"

This time James hesitated. "No one." He turned and looked at his sister. "It's just me and Krissy."

The deputy made an angry sound and pulled his radio off his belt. Even though he turned away, Krissy and James could hear him making a report. "3 bravo 6 to dispatch."

Krissy heard a woman's voice crackle over the radio. "Go 3 bravo 6."

"I've got two kids alone here at the Shepherd house. Does anyone know how to get ahold of the parents?"

"We can call our parents on our cell phones," James called out.

Deputy Howell turned and looked at him and then spoke into his radio again. "Hold on," he said, then held out his hand. Krissy was surprised to see James drop his phone into the deputy's palm but figured James knew what he was doing. The deputy tapped at the phone and then held it near his ear.

Krissy heard her mother's voicemail answer. The deputy made a sound of disgust and hung up without leaving a message. He dialed their dad's number next. He answered right away.

"Hello? James? What's wrong?"

"Mr. Shepherd. I'm sorry to alarm you. This is Dave Howell with the sheriff's office. Your son gave me his phone to call you. We're checking all the houses in the area for the two boys and without an adult here at the house, I can't legally go in."

Krissy could barely hear her dad's response. "I understand. Can you hold on a second?"

"Sure," the deputy answered, and it sounded like the phone call was put on hold. A few seconds later the radio attached to the deputy's shoulder chirped.

The deputy pulled his radio off his shoulder and answered: "3 bravo 6, go."

"3 bravo 6, what's your location?"

"I'm at 200 Shepherd's Lane."

"200 Shepherd's Lane, copy."

The deputy waited another moment and then Krissy heard her dad come back on the phone. "Deputy?"

"Yes, sir," the deputy answered as he snapped his radio back onto his shoulder.

"I'm on my way home. You can search the house now, or you can wait for me. I'm about 30 minutes away."

"Yes, sir. I can wait."

Krissy watched the deputy end the call on James's phone and hand it back to him. "You two go back inside. I'll wait out here."

Krissy and James watched the deputy walk back to his patrol car and went inside as they were told.

They were done eating by the time their dad arrived. Krissy was thrilled to see Grandma Naomi in tow with Justice's grandma right behind her. Even though she wasn't their blood relative, Krissy knew Grandma Naomi loved them. She was just worried about her friend.

Frank let the ladies in first and then motioned for the deputy to come in. They talked quietly at the door and then Frank led him through the entirety of the small house with James following. Krissy went into the kitchen to see Mrs. Guthrie sitting at the table while Grandma Naomi made coffee. When Krissy walked in, Naomi turned and pulled her into a hug and shushed her. Krissy knew she was apologizing for not being there.

"It's OK. We're OK," she said, then felt terrible when Mrs. Guthrie pulled out a tissue and wiped her already wet eyes.

"I'm really sorry about Justice," Krissy said politely.

Mrs. Guthrie didn't answer but nodded her thanks.

When the deputy was done, Krissy's dad saw him off and returned to the kitchen.

"I've got to go back to work." He gave Krissy another hug. "Answer if I call you...text if I text you, OK?"

Krissy nodded and her dad left.

Grandma Naomi made two mugs of coffee and sat down with her friend. Krissy knew they really didn't want her in the kitchen with them, so she wandered into the living room to look for James.

She found him staring out across the fields in front of their house.

"The police think they're dead," he said, his voice toneless.

"How do you know that?" Krissy felt a tightness in her chest.

"I heard him say to Dad that after the first couple of days, if they don't find them, they're most likely looking for bodies. They're searching everybody's basement and shed."

"We don't have a basement or a shed." They didn't have anything at all but a house and a carport that was nothing more than a thin metal roof on four poles.

"We've got a dirt cellar that used to hold coal, but there's nothing there now that the oil tank's outside. Door's under the back steps."

Krissy watched her brother watching the corn sway back and forth. "What was in the cellar?"

James shook his head. "Nothing."

Krissy waited a long time for him to say something else. She was about to turn away when he spoke again.

"We're gonna look at that map tomorrow."

By that evening, it looked like Mrs. Guthrie was there for an extended stay. While Krissy helped Grandma Naomi with dinner, James helped his father set up the small roll-out bed in Grandma Naomi's bedroom. Mrs. Guthrie helped by moving furniture over to make room while Krissy's mom helped by complaining about having another mouth to feed during this trying time.

Krissy was surprised to see her father come out of Naomi's bedroom and grab his wife by the elbow to pull her out of the kitchen. She could see him speaking into her ear, his expression angry. When they came back in, his face was grim and her mother was silent but fuming.

Dinner was a quiet affair, and Krissy and her brother were sent to bed shortly after the dishes were finished.

With all that was going on, it was a long time before Krissy fell asleep.

Ellen

Great. It wasn't bad enough that they had to put up with Naomi, now they had that ancient Lynne Guthrie moping around here.

"You know it's hard enough as it is with the five of us," she snapped. Of course Frank ignored her and moved the roll-out through the kitchen into Naomi's room. "Who's going to go get more groceries? That's what I'd like to know. I've already got my hands full with this kidnap..." Ellen was startled into silence when Frank grabbed her elbow and pulled her into the living room.

"Don't say another word, Ellen. I mean it," Frank whispered. Ellen stared at him in shock. "Lynne Guthrie has been through enough already. She doesn't need you standing here making things worse."

Is he *serious*? Ellen thought. First he lays his hands on her and then he has the nerve to tell her she can't speak her mind in her own home? Ellen pressed her lips so hard she could feel her teeth cutting into the soft tissue of her mouth. She stared after him as he returned to the kitchen and briefly considered just walking out the front door. Unfortunately, her mother wasn't answering her phone, and Ellen didn't want to risk a drive all the way to Northridge to only to have to turn around and come back.

Resigned to suffering in the worst marriage ever, Ellen followed him into the kitchen and reluctantly sat down.

NINE

Krissy

The next morning Krissy woke up to the smell of bacon. She met James in the hallway and the two went downstairs to see Grandma Naomi and Mrs. Guthrie cooking at the stove. Their mother sat at the table with her coffee and she didn't look happy, but for once wasn't saying anything about it.

Krissy slid into her seat and tried to shrink a little bit so her mother wouldn't notice her. Mrs. Guthrie's eyes were wet when she put a plate of scrambled eggs, bacon, and French toast in front of Krissy, who minded her manners and thanked her. Mrs. Guthrie gave her a weak smile and then patted her on the head before returning to the stove to prepare James's plate.

Krissy choked on her eggs when her mother spoke.

"I suppose your father talked to you about staying near the house?"

Krissy and James nodded.

Ellen looked at them like they belonged to some other mother. She seemed to come to a decision, and Krissy was pretty sure she didn't want to know what that decision was. "Well, I'm already late," she announced then grabbed her things and left.

Nobody said good-bye.

Despite her disability, Grandma Naomi monopolized the conversation at the breakfast table. Usually Krissy translated for her, but Mrs. Guthrie seemed to understand her perfectly. When they were finished with their breakfast, Krissy collected plates but was chased away from the sink by Grandma Naomi. When Mrs. Guthrie suggested they go outside and play, Krissy knew she and her grandmother wanted to talk about Justice.

James took advantage of their distraction and went outside. Krissy followed him out and found him staring at his bike as if trying to make a decision.

"We're not allowed to go anywhere," she warned. James seemed to notice her then and sat down hard on the step.

"Clinton still can't leave his house anyway," he grumbled, then sank his chin into his hand.

Krissy pulled a dirty old soccer ball out of the bushes and used it for a seat. She rolled it underneath her, watching her brother struggle with whatever thought was churning through his brain.

"Damn. I wish we had a computer we could use," he blurted.

Krissy nodded in agreement, though she didn't really know what they needed a computer for. They used them during their technology labs at school, but a lot of kids still didn't have computers at home or at least ones they could use. Their dad had an old computer, but Krissy and James weren't allowed to use it unless he was home, and they weren't allowed to play on it at all. It was too slow to be much fun anyway, so Krissy didn't see what all the fuss was about.

James's pocket chirped, startling the both of them. He pulled his phone out and looked at the screen. "It's Dad," he said by way of explanation. He sent a return text letting their dad know that they were home and everything was normal.

Krissy felt bad. She'd left her phone upstairs on her nightstand, and for all she knew, her dad was freaking out because she wasn't answering. She thought about going up and checking it when she and James heard a rustling in the corn behind her. They both turned to see Zach wading through the tall, papered stalks. Pickers would be going through in September, and Krissy knew it would all be cut down late in the year.

"Hey," Zach called out, and Krissy was struck again by how handsome he was. With his black hair and dark eyes, he was way more handsome than most of the guys on TV.

"Hey," James answered, his face mulish.

Grandma Naomi appeared in doorway behind James, suspicion clearly visible on her face.

"Hey, Miss Naomi," Zach smiled at her. "Everything all right?"

Grandma Naomi didn't try to talk to him, so she just nodded. She did consent to give him a small smile, but that was about it.

"Good to hear. Let me know if you need anything." Zach disappeared back into the corn.

Just then a fat raindrop landed smack dab in the middle of Krissy's forehead. Another second later the sky opened up and rain poured down. James and Krissy ran into the house and spent the rest of the day staring out at the storm.

The next day was Saturday, and Krissy's dad drove Mrs. Guthrie home so she could meet with the deputies looking for Justice.

It was also the day they went as a family to visit Grandpa Nate at Spring Haven. Krissy liked Grandpa Nate but hated the hospital. Even though its red brick building was well kept and the lawns were always short and green, the idea that it was filled with crazy people made her nervous. They left early for the hour drive and arrived just as Grandpa Nate was finishing his breakfast. One of the orderlies led them into the activity room where they waited. Already bored, James and Krissy started working on the bazillion-piece puzzle scattered across the table. It was only another minute when Grandpa Nate walked in with an elderly woman following close behind him, her hand clutching the back of his shirt. Krissy was surprised that when he sat, she sat right next to him. Krissy glanced at Grandma Naomi, who looked furious. She could tell that her parents were confused too. Grandpa Nate sensed their confusion and gave a small chuckle.

"That's just Joan," he said by way of explanation. "She thinks I'm her late husband."

Just then Joan leaned over and tugged at Grandpa Nate's sleeve. "Bill? Who are these people and why are we sitting with them?"

Grandpa Nate put his hand on hers and squeezed it. "They're family, Joan. It's fine." He turned back to see Grandma Naomi shushing at him, her face thunderous.

Frank tried to mediate, and when that failed, turned the conversation to the missing boys.

"...so Lynne Guthrie was with us for a bit but went back to see if the deputies had anything new to report."

"I'm just glad it wasn't the other Harper boy," Grandpa Nate said. "Pat Harper already had problems. Losing one boy put her in here for almost six months. I can't imagine what she'd do if she lost the other one."

"Mrs. Harper was in here?" Krissy blurted, then shut up when James kicked her under the table. He pushed a handful of puzzle pieces in front of her and put his head down. Krissy followed suit and held her breath until the adults started talking again.

"Pat's always had a problem with the alcohol," Grandpa Nate said, inadvertently answering Krissy's question. "Honestly, it's a wonder she can function at all. She told us some crazy stories when she was in here."

Krissy closed her eyes and crossed her fingers, hoping someone would ask the question she was dying to ask.

"What kind of stories?" Her father had come through for her.

"Things like how the young one...what was his name? Kirk? He was her favorite, and how hard it was for her other son when he disappeared. He was in here too for a while. I think he tried to kill himself. That apple didn't fall far from the mama tree." Grandpa Nate's friend Joan tugged at his sleeve, but this time he ignored her. Grandma Naomi shot daggers at the other woman but kept quiet.

"The older one was always a bit of a problem, though. I remember when he set fire to one of Harper's cornfields. It took two counties to put it out. Smelled for days. Can't imagine how bad his ass hurt after Harper lit him up."

"I don't remember Kirk being a problem," Frank said. Krissy's mom made a comment about the appropriateness of the conversation, but Grandpa Nate interrupted her.

"He was always kind of sickly...or was that the older one? I can't remember."

"Kirk was in my boy scout troop," Frank said slowly as if he was still thinking. "I don't remember anything being wrong with him."

"Must have been the other one then," Grandpa said dismissively, then launched into a new conversation about the food.

They stayed for an hour and offered to take Grandpa Nate to lunch somewhere other than the hospital. He declined as usual, and Krissy wondered if it was because he was really afraid of leaving the hospital or if he was afraid the hospital wouldn't let him back in.

They said their good-byes and left Grandpa standing at the door to his ward, Joan swaying just behind him, his shirt still clutched in her hand.

On the ride back home, Grandma Naomi was more silent than usual, and Krissy could see the wheels turning in her mind. She was really upset, and Krissy didn't know what to say to make her feel better.

Instead, James spoke up. "That Joan was so weird, right? Why does she hold on to Grandpa Nate like that?"

Ellen shot James a look, but Frank answered. "I don't think she really knows who Grandpa Nate is. I think she's a confused lady and Grandpa Nate doesn't want to upset her."

Krissy could tell by Grandma Naomi's face that she wasn't buying that explanation. She was Grandpa's third wife for a reason.

The rest of the trip passed in silence, so Krissy fell asleep.

It was raining again by the time they got home. Frank picked up hamburgers on the way so Grandma Naomi wouldn't have to cook. He could tell she was still upset. Dinner was a silent affair and when it was done, Krissy helped clean up so that her father could take Grandma Naomi back to Justice's house. Her mother went upstairs and James and her dad went into the living room to watch TV.

Krissy wasn't interested in the game they were watching, so she went upstairs to her room. Even though her door was closed, Krissy could hear her mother talking on the phone.

"Did you know? I had no idea Pat Harper was such a mess. I mean I knew she drank but not so much she had to be hospitalized for it...I know! And I didn't even know they had another son. I thought they just had Jeremy. It sounds like he's as much a mess as his mother. Did you know he was committed to Spring Haven for trying to kill himself? I wonder if it was because of the Jacobsens. You didn't hear about that? Oh my God...so apparently he was caught peeping in the Jacobsen's window. But get this, when they caught him, he was looking in the wrong window. He was looking in Matt's window, not Heather's. So stupid. Just like his mother."

Krissy couldn't hear what her mother said next, her voice was too low. She pressed her ear against the wall but could only hear mumbling. She moved to the floor and pressed her ear to the wall vent. Her mother's voice was low, but she could make out her words.

"And she's a complete mess. The last time I went over there she was still wearing her bathrobe...in the middle of the afternoon. And I swear she didn't have a thing on underneath. No wonder that weirdo Zach likes it there so much. It can't be because of Tom...crazy Holy Roller. Oh, Frank's coming up, I've got to go."

Krissy jumped up off the floor and crawled under her covers. She grabbed her cell phone and started playing one of the games her dad had put on it. A second later, her dad tapped on her door, opened it slightly, and stuck his head in.

"Everything OK?" he asked. Krissy nodded.

"Make sure you're charging your phone every night, OK?" he said and Krissy nodded again. Her father gave her a sad smile and shut the door.

Next door she could hear him ask her mother who she had been talking to. Even though she couldn't hear the answer, Krissy was pretty sure her mother lied to her father. Their words weren't clear, but Krissy could tell they were fighting. It went on for a long time and it wasn't until she heard the front door slam that she got up to put on her pajamas and crawl under the covers. She knew without looking that her mom had walked out.

Ellen

God, he's an asshole, Ellen fumed. If she hadn't walked out without her keys she'd be driving away right now. Instead she dropped down hard on the front step and pouted. She could hear someone moving around in the house behind her, but couldn't tell if it was Frank or Naomi.

Ellen sat, listening closely for the sound of Frank coming to apologize for yelling at her. Every time it sounded like the door was about to open, she tensed, readying herself for another confrontation. She wasn't about to let him off the hook without telling him where he could stuff his apology. Ellen waited, certain that he was going to step outside any minute. She listened to the house settling down behind her. Ellen knew there was no way he was going to go to bed without her. He'd be out on his ass if he did. He was coming. She was certain of it...any minute now.

TEN

Krissy

Krissy was suffering a fitful sleep when a quiet thump woke her up. Disoriented, she looked around her room until she saw the clock glowing in the corner and heard another thump like someone had missed a step on the stairs. She glanced at the clock and saw it was way past midnight.

Krissy sat up and listened carefully. Someone was stepping into the hallway. Krissy quietly crept out of bed and opened her door a crack, where she saw her mother standing in the dark of the hallway, her ear pressed against her closed bedroom door. Krissy was glad her mother faced away from her. She really didn't want to get yelled at. She slowly closed her door and listened as her mother made her way back downstairs. When the house was silent again, Krissy went back to bed.

Late the next morning, when Krissy woke up, everyone was gone. If she hadn't seen Mr. Harper driving his tractor off in the distance, she would have thought the world had ended without her. Maybe it had and they were the only two people left. She hoped he was a good cook because she was hungry. But first she needed to pee.

Krissy was just drying her hands when she heard the back door slam. Suddenly nervous, she stepped out of the bathroom and stood at the top of the stairs, listening. Someone was walking around in the kitchen.

"James?" Krissy called out quietly.

"Yeah?" he called back, and she exhaled the breath she didn't know she'd been holding.

Krissy trotted down the stairs and walked into the kitchen to see James digging in the refrigerator.

"Where did you go?" she asked.

"Just to the end of the driveway," he answered from inside the fridge.

"I thought you weren't going to leave me by myself," she said, annoyed that her voice sounded whiny and babyish.

"I'm not," he answered, then pulled out the milk. "I was just checking to see if there was another sheriff's car parked there again. Don't we have anything besides cereal?"

"You want peanut butter toast?" she asked, and he nodded. Krissy went to get the bread and peanut butter out of the pantry. "Why were you looking for the sheriff?"

"I don't want them seeing us when we leave," he answered, then poured them both a glass of milk.

Krissy looked at her brother. "Where are we going?"

"Library," he answered. "Do we have any chocolate syrup?"

"No, just powder," she answered, then turned to pull the toast out of the toaster. "Why are we going to the library?" she asked as she spread the peanut butter and placed the slices on a plate. She handed James his plate and turned to make her own toast.

"Clinton's gonna meet us at the library with that map." James took a bite out of his toast. "Somehow we gotta find out where Mason and Justice are."

Krissy sat silently and wondered how a bunch of kids were going to find Mason and Justice when the police couldn't.

When they were done with their breakfast, James helped her with the dishes and they set off.

They rode their bikes down to the end of the driveway, James going slow so Krissy could keep up on the gravel. At the end, James stopped and peered around the wall of corn to see if the sheriff had left a patrol car there again, but the road was empty. James and Krissy pedaled their bikes onto the blacktop where it was easier to ride and took off down the road.

The library was far for James and Krissy since they lived the farthest away. Even taking farm roads and side roads, it took them half an hour to get there. Krissy was hot and sweaty by the time they parked their bikes outside. Inside the library was cool, and Krissy was grateful for the air-conditioning.

There were a surprising number of people there, mostly moms with younger children looking for something to do to ease the boredom of summer. Krissy and James walked to the back and staked out a table in the reference section. A few minutes later, Minor and Clinton walked in followed by a kid named Lucas who James knew from school. Krissy felt weird being the only girl but figured if she kept her mouth shut, they wouldn't object to her being there.

"Hey," Clinton called out, quietly so as not to raise the ire of the reference librarian. Krissy wondered why he was being so careful. The library was already noisy from all the little kids running around.

"Hey," James answered. "How did you get out? I thought your mom wasn't letting you go anywhere."

"My grandma had to go back to work, so my mom got our neighbor to come stay. She's like a hundred and all she does is sleep all day. She won't even know I'm gone."

Krissy stared at Clinton and wondered why her mother didn't think Clinton was good-looking enough to kidnap. He looked fine to her. She wondered if the other boys who disappeared were good-looking, too. If Kirk Harper looked anything like his dad, not so much, she thought.

Clinton unfolded the map and Minor and Lucas helped spread it across the table. He'd already marked it up and Krissy wondered why. It looked old and some of the marks were different from the others.

"I found this map in my dad's stuff. I'm pretty sure these are from the first time kids went missing," he said, pointing to the faded red dots scattered on the map. "These blue ones are mine. This is where Mason went missing and since we don't really know where Justice disappeared, I put it near where his house is."

"When I left Justice he was only a couple of blocks from his house," Minor said. "So that's probably about right."

"We should probably mark where everybody lives, too," Lucas recommended. "Is there a way of finding out where the other kids lived?"

"Kirk Harper lived near me," James said and pointed to a spot on the map that approximated the Harper's farm. Clinton made a small blue mark then wrote the letter H next to it. Krissy assumed this meant "house."

"And one of them...the Tucker kid, lived around the corner from me," Minor added. "His parents still live there." He looked for a moment and then pointed to another spot on the map, and Clinton made another mark.

"We still don't know about the other two," Clinton said, but no one had any suggestions on how to find out about the other two boys. Instead, they stared at the map. Krissy looked down, too, and noticed that her house was almost in the middle of all the marks. Her chest started to hurt in a weird way, but she didn't want to say anything about it to James in front of his friends.

"I wonder if anyone else has ever gone missing around here," she said instead.

Clinton looked at her for a second and then shrugged. "I don't know. I don't think so. We can at least start thinking about how we're going to find Mason and Justice. For now I think we need to look in all the places in between the dots."

"The red dots or the blue dots?" Minor asked.

"All of them," Clinton answered.

They were so busy formulating a plan that they didn't notice they had company until a shadow fell across the map. Krissy looked up to see Deputy Howell standing over them. She nudged James, who looked up and then stopped Clinton with a gesture. Everyone fell silent and stared at the deputy.

"What are you kids doing here?" he asked. "Where are your parents?"

"They're around," Clinton answered. "We're just looking at stuff."

"Around where?" Deputy Howell asked. "Because the librarian didn't see any moms or dads come in with you."

Rather than lie, everyone kept silent.

"That's what I thought," Deputy Howell said, his tone more sad than angry. "What's with the map?" he asked, then leaned over and looked at it. It only took a second for him to realize what all the dots meant. "Where did you get this?"

"It was my dad's," Clinton answered. "We're just trying to figure things out."

"I knew your dad," Deputy Howell said quietly. "He wouldn't want you trying to figure this out on your own, you know. And he definitely wouldn't want you running around when kids have gone missing."

Clinton looked away, and Krissy thought he might be about to cry.

"I want you guys to go home right now," Deputy Howell said. "And I'm going to drive by and check that you're there."

Everyone moved to get up. Clinton reached out to fold up his map when Deputy Howell slid it away from him. "I'm going to borrow this, OK?" he asked. "I'll bring it by your house once I photocopy it."

Clinton's face looked hurt and angry, but he held his tongue and just nodded.

"Go on, now," Deputy Howell ordered and they went.

Outside they all grabbed their bikes and were about to ride away when Clinton stopped them.

"We should see each other home," he said. "Minor's house is closest, then Lucas, then me, then James and Krissy'll have to watch each other."

"We got phones in case we get in trouble," Krissy said, and James nodded.

"Cool," Clinton looked impressed. "Let's go, then."

The ride took much longer with all the side trips to see the other boys home, and by the time Krissy and James reached Clinton's road, Krissy was worn out. Luckily Clinton didn't live that far away from them, so it was only another mile or so before they'd be home.

"James?" Krissy asked as they pedaled away from Clinton's house. "Why did that deputy say he knew Clinton's dad?"

"Because he was a cop, too." James panted, "They probably worked together."

"How did his dad die?"

"He was in a car accident," James answered.

Krissy thought that was really sad. Even though Justice was the best-looking out of James's friends, Clinton was the nicest. He was really smart and he never treated Krissy like an annoying little kid like the other boys sometimes did.

They rode the rest of the way home in silence, not because they didn't have anything to say but because they were so darn tired...so tired that Krissy almost rode in front of an old pickup truck coming up behind them fast. If the driver hadn't honked she would have been roadkill. As it was, he glared at her as he passed by and didn't even smile when Krissy waved an apology. Once they got to their driveway, Krissy got off her bike. Rather than try to ride on the gravel that covered their driveway, she walked the rest of the way, pushing her bike along, then stopped in the grass in front of the house and just about fell over. James dropped his bike next to hers, sprawled out on the grass, and closed his eyes. Krissy sat down on the step and thanked Jesus that the front of the house was shady.

"You hungry?" she asked after a time and hoped James would say no. He didn't disappoint and moved his head from side to side from the ground.

Krissy closed her eyes and let the cicadas hypnotize her. She eventually started dozing when James woke her up.

"What's all that?" he asked, listening to the sound of gravel popping. Mr. Harper's corn was so high that they couldn't see down their own driveway anymore.

Krissy was about to say she didn't know when Deputy Howell's patrol car appeared and came to a hard stop, followed by a cloud of dust.

"Is Clinton here with you?" he asked, and Krissy and James shook their heads.

"We saw him to his street and then we came home," James answered. "Why?"

"Did you see him go inside his house?" Deputy Howell's tone was scaring Krissy. She felt tears burning her eyes.

"We saw him go up his driveway. He said he had to put his bike in the garage or his mom would run it over. Why?" James asked again, this time his voice shaking.

Instead of answering, Deputy Howell pulled his radio up to his mouth and turned away.

Krissy burst into tears.

Ellen

She was still in the fitting room when her cell phone went off, startling her. Technically she was off for lunch and not really doing anything wrong. She was entitled to take a lunch and it was none of their business how she spent her break.

Ellen pulled her own skirt on and reached over and pulled her phone from her purse. If this was Rick calling to give her grief about going over on her lunch time, well, let's just say she was ready to give him an earful. She could be at a doctor's appointment for all he knew.

Ellen looked at her phone and saw that she had not just one missed call, but seven. Who on earth was calling her seven times? One call was from James, which Ellen dismissed immediately. James knew better than to bother her during the day and must have dialed by accident. The other six were from Frank, who should also know better but was acting like such an ass lately that nothing surprised Ellen anymore. Of course just as she was deleting her call log, her phone rang again. Ellen hesitated and then answered it.

"What?" Ellen barked.

"Where are you, Ellen?" Frank asked, his tone perilously close to yelling at her.

"Where do you think I am?" Ellen answered. "I'm at work."

"I called the hospital when you didn't answer your phone. They said you were at lunch."

"So? I can't eat lunch?" Ellen pulled her blouse over her head and pulled on her shoes.

Of course he ignored her question. "You need to get home right now," Frank ordered, and Ellen bristled.

"I can't do that, Frank. I've got to get back to the office." Ellen didn't really have an office, but she liked the way it sounded, and Frank didn't know any better.

"Another one of James's friends had gone missing and the police are at the house. You need to get there as quickly as you can."

"Uh, why don't you leave your job and go?" Ellen griped. "I have work to do."

"Just go home, Ellen. I'm leaving here as soon as I can."

Ellen stared at her phone in shock. Frank had hung up on her. Still stunned, she walked out of the Kohl's fitting room and then the front door without her purchases. The hospital would just have to understand. This was a family emergency, after all.

ELEVEN

Krissy

Somewhere in the minutes between Krissy and James dropping him off and Deputy Howell showing up to return his map, Clinton had disappeared. His bike was in the garage and the garage door was closed, but Clinton never walked into the house.

This time the small house was filled with sheriff's deputies and even some state police. Another group of men stood outside the Shepherd home. Krissy couldn't tell who they were; they all looked the same in their dark blue windbreakers.

When Krissy's father came home, it was to find his wife scowling in the corner with her arms crossed in front of her, James being grilled for the hundredth time, and Krissy sitting silently, staring at everyone, her face so wet with tears she looked like she was standing under a shower.

She was so grateful when her father crossed the small living room to pick her up and hold her close. Her silent tears erupted into full-blown sobbing, so loud it reminded everyone else in the room that she was still there. Except her mother. Her mother knew all along and Krissy had been the target of at least half her anger.

Krissy's dad carried her into the kitchen and sat her on the counter next to the sink to bathe Krissy's face with a cold, wet paper towel. Her mother had followed them in and stood nearby, quietly raving.

"I can't even, Frank. I just can't. You're going to have to figure out what you're going to do. I can't keep coming home and finding the house turned upside down because these two can't keep track of their friends."

"Be quiet, Ellen," Frank said quietly.

"Don't tell me to be quiet," Ellen snapped. "You think you can walk in here at the eleventh hour and miss being accused of neglect and look like the hero picking up our daughter when you should be punishing her and her idiot brother for leaving the house when they weren't..."

"I SAID BE QUIET," Frank yelled, finally getting her attention. Ellen's mouth fell open and she and Krissy both stared at him. Frank lowered his voice. "Your first priority should be these kids, but it's not. You could take time off from your job and stay here with them, but you don't. You have always put yourself first and it's time you think about someone else for a change."

"I NEED TO WORK, *FRANK*," Ellen countered. "You think this family survives on your income alone?"

Krissy heard her father take a deep breath as if steeling himself to finally confront his wife.

"You don't provide a dime to the family income and you know it. You don't even buy the kids' things. I know you've been either shopping or sending your paychecks to your mother and your idiot brother, both of whom have jobs of their own," he said, his voice low and angry.

"I'll have you know Jerry is *not* working anymore," Ellen snapped. "He's had some health issues and had to take a leave of absence from the bakery. He's staying with my mother now while he recovers, so yes, he does need my help, not that it's any business of *yours*."

"It is my business when our children are left unattended. You're their *mother*. You should be here taking care of them. You should *want* to take care of them."

"You think I can just waltz in and tell my boss I need time off? They'll *fire* me, Frank," Ellen responded. "Rick's just looking for a way to get rid of me."

"I'm not surprised after the stunt you pulled with those files," Frank said. "You deserve to be fired."

Ellen's mouth fell open. "I can't believe you just said that. I make a nice home for you here. I gave you beautiful children. So beautiful I'm surprised they haven't been kidnapped yet..."

"GODDAMN IT, ELLEN, DO YOU EVEN LISTEN TO YOURSELF? WHAT IS WRONG WITH YOU?"

Krissy burst into tears again, but whether it was from her mother's words or her father's outburst she didn't know.

Frank seemed to realize Krissy was still there and picked her up as Deputy Howell appeared in the doorway.

"Is everything OK in here?" he asked, his eye on Krissy and her father.

"This is a family issue," Ellen snapped as Frank answered, "No, everything is not OK."

Deputy Howell looked uncomfortable.

"I'm sorry, Mr. and Mrs. Shepherd, but I can't emphasize enough how important it is to have someone stay here with Krissy and James."

Krissy's father sighed. "I'll go get Naomi. She needs to understand that she *has* to stay here."

Deputy Howell looked even more uncomfortable.

"Um, I'm not sure that's possible," he said. "One of our guys went over to the Guthrie's to bring her back here and she was gone. Lynne Guthrie told me Miss Naomi checked herself into Spring Haven."

Krissy and her parents stared at him in surprise.

"What?" Frank asked. "Why?"

Deputy Howell shrugged. "Depression is what Mrs. Guthrie said. We called over there and she's committed herself."

"Oh, for Christ's sake," Ellen muttered and looked away.

Krissy's father wiped his hand down his face and then looked at her. She felt sorry for her father. In the span of five minutes he looked a hundred years older.

"Then their mother will have to stay," he said quietly, then quelled her with a look when she started to raise an objection.

Deputy Howell looked relieved.

Ellen stared at her husband and then turned and stomped out of the kitchen.

Ellen

Unbelievable, Ellen thought to herself as she slammed her bedroom door behind her. If Frank thought he scored any points with anyone trying to act like the loving father everyone knew he wasn't, he was delusional.

Ellen grabbed the phone from the nightstand and dialed her mother. She sat in silence, listening to it ring and ring and ring, knowing her mother had call waiting and was most likely on the other line.

Ellen hung up and gave her a minute. Since she called her mother every day, it made her even angrier that her mother hadn't kept her line free for her call, especially now when it was urgent.

Ellen sat and hit redial over and over until her mother finally picked up.

"Jesus Christ, Ellen," her mother ranted. "What's so important that you can't even let me finish my call?"

Ellen was pissed that her mother didn't even say hello first but let it go.

"I'm having problems here at home and I need to come stay with you for a while," she replied, opting for a tone that was both angry and despondent.

"Why?" her mother asked. "What's happening?"

"It's Frank," Ellen answered. "With all that's going on with these stupid kids going missing, he's expecting me to just leave my job and stay home with Krissy and James."

"So?"

Ellen stared at the phone. At the least her mother could take her side in this.

"*Soooo*, I can't just leave my job," Ellen replied, trying to keep the sarcasm out of her voice. If there was one thing that would piss off her mother, it was sarcasm. "Rick is dying to get rid of me. Frank's just not being reasonable. Those kids have him convinced that they're not safe here by themselves."

"Well, where's Naomi?" her mother asked. "Shouldn't she be there watching them?"

"Naomi checked herself into Spring Haven," Ellen sighed. "Even she doesn't want to be here."

"Well, I don't know what to tell you, but you can't come here. I've already got my hands full with your brother and I don't need anything else on my plate right now."

"It's not like I need you to take care of me, *Mom*." Ellen didn't bother with her tone this time. "*I* haven't gone crazy. I just can't stay here with Frank constantly up my butt. Let him stay home if it's so damn important to him."

"Well, I don't know about that, Ellen," her mother replied, her tone sounding perilously close to patronizing and dismissive. "He does make more money than you do."

"That's hardly the point, *Mother*," Ellen responded in kind, aggravated that their conversation wasn't moving in the direction she wanted it to. "My job has potential for growth; his doesn't. I think it's pretty obvious who has a career and who has just a job. Besides, I'm sure Jerry's just taking up space in his room. I can just take my old room back."

"I told you, Ellen," her mother said firmly. "I don't have the room for both of you. If you can't stay home, then hire a babysitter."

"Jesus Christ, Mom." Ellen was losing her temper. "I can't afford that. I'd just be paying the babysitter my paycheck. I might as well stay home."

"There, then," her mother answered, sounding supremely satisfied at the conversation coming to the appropriate conclusion. "Problem solved."

Ellen stared at the phone. Her mother had hung up on her. Worse yet, Frank was opening their door.

TWELVE

Krissy

Krissy was exhausted from all the crying when her father carried her up to her room. She was grateful when he laid her on her bed and pulled her quilt over her. And she loved him when he leaned over and kissed her goodnight.

She closed her eyes and listened to him go into the other room and yell at her mother. Krissy didn't care what they were saying, though. It was probably the same things they had said downstairs.

All Krissy knew was if Clinton was taken and, according to her mother at least, wasn't that good-looking, she and James were in trouble. Big trouble.

Krissy got out of bed and went to her desk. It took a little bit if searching but eventually her hand fell on the cool metal of her old school scissors. Krissy carried them over to her mirror. She stared at her reflection for a long time. Then she pulled her long, brown hair away from her face and began to cut.

The next morning Frank did stay home. Krissy was surprised to find him making pancakes. She was even more surprised to see her mother sitting at the table, fuming.

She sidled past her mother's chair and went to the cabinet to fetch plates and glasses for breakfast.

When her father turned to wish her a good morning, he stopped short, stunned at the sight of his daughter.

"Krissy, honey?" he asked carefully. "What did you do to your hair?"

Krissy set the table and took her seat. "I cut it so it wouldn't be pretty anymore," she whispered.

Her father's lips pressed into a grim line, and he glared at his wife but didn't say anything.

James walked in a minute later and stopped in the doorway, obviously surprised to see both parents still home. He moved carefully past his mother, pulled the milk from the fridge, and sat at the table. He started at the sight of Krissy's hair but didn't say anything. She knew he'd be quizzing her about it later.

"We're going to go visit Naomi at the hospital and see if we can't get her to come back home," Frank announced as he placed a plate full of pancakes in the center of the table.

Krissy glanced at her mother, who just glared at the pile of golden buttermilk pancakes like they were made of dog poo. She wasn't surprised when her mother got up abruptly and left the room.

Krissy's father sat down heavily and sighed. "You know your mother loves you, right?" he asked quietly, and Krissy could tell even he didn't believe it.

"No, she doesn't," James replied with his mouth full.

Frank looked at his son. "Why would you say that, bud? Of course she loves you."

Krissy could tell her brother didn't want to answer that question. She didn't really want to think about it at all. It hurt too much.

James shrugged. "If she loved us she'd be worried about us. She wouldn't be saying things about how we're so pretty that we should be kidnapped, too. It's like she wants it to happen." James's voice broke and Krissy's heart went out to him. She was close to crying herself. So close that she didn't trust herself to sound normal if she said anything, so she just nodded.

Frank reached over and put his hand on James's shoulder and squeezed, which only made it harder for her brother to not cry.

"I'm sorry, James," Frank said quietly. "I know this has been the hardest for you. Those boys are your friends and you're worried about them. I understand. But I need you to stay here. No matter what, you can't keep going out."

Krissy watched her brother not promise, and her heart sank. She wasn't hungry anymore, so she pushed her plate away and asked to be excused.

Upstairs she could hear mother on the phone again and it sounded like she was asking to stay at Grandma's. Rather than listen in, Krissy closed her door softly and went to sit in front of her window.

Things weren't always like this. Though her mother was never very loving or affectionate, she wasn't always this mean. When they lived in the apartment in Springfield, their mom stayed home and took care of them while their dad worked. There were other moms there for her to visit with so she always had something to do and someone to talk to, even when Krissy and James were in school.

But when Grandpa Nate checked himself into Spring Haven, they moved here to help with the bills. Krissy knew her mother wanted her own house instead of an apartment, but this house wasn't exactly what she had in mind. Ellen wanted to live on North Fountain, but those houses were super expensive. There was no way her family could ever afford to live there.

Krissy didn't know why her mother changed, but she knew when. It happened as soon as she started working at the medical center.

Krissy knew her mother felt important there, but she also knew that people didn't really like her. When they were supposed to be asleep, Krissy would listen to her mother complain that her coworkers were getting together without inviting her. They even had a Christmas party at The Hickory, which was supposed to be the nicest restaurant in town, but Ellen didn't find out about it until the day after.

If she was really honest with herself, Krissy probably wouldn't invite her mother, either. It was just too embarrassing when she started complaining. And her mother had this thing that she did to waiters and waitresses. Her dad called it putting on airs, but in Krissy's mind her mother made sure that people knew they were beneath her no matter who they were. Ellen would send waiters running for new forks, or cleaner napkins, or a fresh bottle of ketchup, and if she saw a spot on something she always made a really big deal about it. She would be rude no matter how hard they were trying and it made Krissy want to be extra nice. She knew her father felt the same way because he always left extra money on the table when

her mother wasn't looking. She was the reason they never went anywhere anymore.

Krissy stared out at Mr. Harper's farm and watched as a figure
moved back and forth across the property. She wondered if it was Zach
and hoped he was OK. It would be horrible if something bad happened
to him. Then she wouldn't have anyone to marry.

A knock at the door brought her back to the present. Krissy's father
poked his head in.

"Get dressed and we'll go get your hair evened out before we go see
Grandpa and Grandma, OK?"

Krissy nodded and got up to change when he closed the door.

Ellen

God, will this never end? Ellen asked herself as she burrowed through
her closet. First Frank makes her take a day off, which *of course* Rick
was more than happy to approve. Then Krissy shows up at the breakfast
table looking like trailer trash with head lice. And now they're going to
drive all day to try to convince Naomi to come home when everyone
knows that's not going to happen.

She was still looking for something presentable to wear when Frank
stuck his head in and told her he was taking Krissy to Supercuts to fix
the mess she'd made of herself. Ellen didn't bother to nod and Frank
didn't bother to acknowledge her lack of response. When she heard the
front door slam, she sat down on the bed and stared at herself in the
mirror.

THIRTEEN

Krissy

Krissy was excited to be going to Supercuts with her dad. She'd never been there, though she knew that's where her mother got her hair done. Usually Grandma Naomi trimmed Krissy's hair. But today she was officially going to get her hair "done," and even though it was just to fix the mess she'd made, it was still pretty cool.

There weren't many people there on a weekday, so Krissy was seated in a chair right away. The hair stylist fussed over her poor hair for a minute and then set about evening up all the weird lengths Krissy had left. When she was done, Krissy's hair had been cut into a short pixie, which only made her small face smaller and her dark brown eyes look huge.

"You look like a little elf girl," the lady said when she turned Krissy around to face the mirror. Krissy stared at herself. She had to agree. She looked just like Tinkerbell without the bun on top...and with brown hair...and brown eyes. Well, maybe not Tinkerbell, but she definitely looked better.

"It's a good thing you didn't chop the top of your hair so short, or this might not have ended up so well," the stylist said, then took the cape off of Krissy. "Now no more playing beauty shop on yourself, OK?"

Krissy nodded and slid out of the chair and ran to her father. Frank looked up and gave her a big smile.

"Well, that looks really nice, doesn't it?" he asked, and Krissy agreed. She stared at herself in the reflection of the window and played with the wisps of hair that curved around her ears. When he had paid, they left for home.

James was waiting for them when they stepped into the kitchen. He laughed when he saw Krissy's hair but stopped when their father glared at him. When their mother walked in everyone held their breath while she dispassionately gave Krissy the once-over.

"It could be worse," Ellen said, and everyone let out a sigh of relief. Krissy knew it wasn't a compliment, but since it was her mother, she didn't really expect one. Except maybe her mother could point out that her new haircut made her eyes look really big and pretty, or her hair looked healthier without all the dry dead ends. Or that she looked really nice. Any of those would have been OK.

Instead, her mother kept her silence, and they all piled into the car for their trip to Spring Haven.

It was too early for lunch and too late for breakfast, so they met with Grandpa Nate and Grandma Naomi in the TV room. There were a lot of other people there when they walked in, and Krissy wondered what was wrong with them. Except for one lady in the corner talking to herself, everyone else looked pretty normal.

"Well, look at you," Grandpa Nate remarked at the sight of Krissy's hair. "For a second I was gonna ask James how he got so much shorter."

Grandma Naomi frowned and shushed over Krissy's hair and then gave her a hug. But as soon as she saw Joan moving closer to try to take her place next to Grandpa Nate, she let go and sat down quickly, giving the other woman a glare.

"Bill?" Joan said plaintively. "I want to sit down. Why won't she let me sit down?" Joan hovered nearby, plucking at Grandpa Nate's sleeve until one of the orderlies came to get her.

"Why can't I sit down, too?" Joan asked the young man. Krissy didn't hear his answer, but she was glad to see Joan go away.

Everyone sat down at the puzzle table and James started picking out pieces just to have something to do.

"We've got a problem at home, Pops," Frank began. "The thing with the missing kids is getting worse and now another one of James's friends went missing just after he and Krissy saw him home. With both of us working, we really need Naomi to come back home."

Krissy watched as Grandma Naomi made angry noises while pointing at the door Joan left through. She could tell that Grandma Naomi was insisting that if she left Spring Haven then Grandpa Nate would have to come home, too. Krissy wondered how they were all going to fit in that tiny house.

"Now calm yourself down, woman," Grandpa Nate scolded. "Joan's harmless and you know it. The poor woman wouldn't know her husband from an armchair."

Krissy could tell Grandma Naomi wasn't buying it.

"I don't know about coming home, Frank," Grandpa Nate shook his head. "We got a great setup here and Medicare pays for everything as long as we have something wrong with us."

"But you don't have anything wrong with you," Krissy's mother snapped. "And even if you did, you could just as easily 'get better' at home where you can watch the kids."

Grandpa Nate narrowed his eyes at Krissy's mother. Krissy knew Grandpa Nate didn't like her mother, but she didn't know why. Probably for the same reasons everyone else didn't like her.

"We have our reasons for staying and with Naomi here suffering from her depression, there's no reason for us to come home until she's feeling better."

"She looks like she's feeling fine to me," Ellen snapped. "She needs to come back to the house with us today so Frank and I can get back to work. Someone has to pay the bills, you know."

Krissy knew her mother was pushing her luck even if her mother didn't know it. She wasn't surprised to see Grandpa Nate's expression turn sly.

"And what bills are you paying exactly?" he asked, even though it wasn't a question. "Seems to me the only bill you're paying is your mother's note on that new car."

Ellen shut her mouth and fumed while Grandpa Nate smirked. "That's what I thought." He turned back to his son. "I'm sorry, Frank, but we're staying put for the time being. Since it won't hurt you none, I suggest your woman stay home to take care of her kids like a normal mother."

Krissy turned to see her father nodding soberly and her mother looking furious. It made her sad in a way that was never going to get better.

They only spent a few more minutes with Grandpa Nate and Grandma Naomi and then left for the long drive home.

Krissy fell asleep minutes into their drive and awoke only when the car had stopped. She opened her eyes and saw James asleep in the seat next to her, the medical center looming in the window behind him.

"Why are we here?" she asked her father, who sat silently in the front seat.

"Your mom needs to let them know she's taking some time off," he answered.

Krissy didn't think that was going to go well.

Ellen

Ellen was furious, as usual. Not only had she endured another ridiculous visit with Frank's father in a facility that reeked of piss and vegetable soup, but now she had to beg that asshole Rick to give her time off to babysit her own children. Luckily Frank stayed in the car with the kids, or he too would have been witness to her humiliation. And knowing Frank, he would have enjoyed it.

Ellen made her way into the building but stopped in a little-used hallway to try to calm herself down before going in to Rick's office. Her heart raced and she could feel her hands trembling. She'd never been so angry before. Thank God she wasn't a crier. There was nothing more embarrassing than being an angry ugly crier.

When she felt settled enough, she walked the hallway and took a right into the administrative section. She poked her head into Rick's office, but he wasn't in there. *Probably lording it over the scheduling staff*, Ellen thought to herself as she made her way to the front patient area. She was surprised to find that Rick wasn't there either.

"Are you looking for Rick?" she heard someone ask behind her. She didn't realize Missy had come in behind her. "He's in the executive offices."

Ellen barely acknowledged the information but turned and headed toward the back of the unit to take the back stairs up. Though Rick managed the unit, he shared his office suite with the rest of the unit's administrative staff—like billing and credentialing—while the chief administrator and chief of clinical staff all had suites on the floor above. Ellen had always found this grossly unfair since she and the other women in her office all worked ten times harder than the fat old men upstairs, and they were relegated to cubicles and minimal pay.

They even got nicer furniture, and Ellen begrudged them every stick of wood. There wasn't anyone sitting at the main reception desk, so she stepped back and followed the sound of Rick's annoying laugh. She could tell he was somewhere near the conference rooms, so she headed in that direction. When she found him, he was giggling with a woman Ellen barely recognized and didn't care why or how she recognized her.

Trying for a conciliatory tone, and failing, Ellen blurted his name.

"Rick? I need a minute with you," she said, then cursed herself for sounding like a bitch. Well, it was his fault he brought out the worst in her.

Rick looked surprised to see her. "Oh, Ellen," he said, trying to sound polite for the benefit of the woman sitting next to him. "I thought you were taking today off."

"Yeah, well, I need to talk to you about that," she answered, still hovering in the doorway.

"Come in, then," Rick said and waved to a chair nearby. "You remember Diane Miller, right?"

"Sure," Ellen answered, trying not to sound like she couldn't care less who the other woman was. She really didn't want to sit down with them, so she just moved a little closer to the conference table. "Listen, this thing with the missing kids has gotten much more serious for my family and the police are sure they're the next target, so I've been asked to stay home with them to make sure they're protected. It's an official request, you know, not one that I can just ignore."

Rick nodded seriously and even had the nerve to look concerned. *Like he really cares*, Ellen thought.

"Of course, your family, your children, are your first priority. We certainly understand why you need to leave us."

Ellen shook her head. *What bullshit*, she thought. Of course he was going to act like she was quitting.

"I'm not *leaving*," she countered. "I'm trying to tell you the police are making me stay home. I'm planning on coming back as soon as all of this is done."

Rick and what's-her-name looked at each other gravely, and Ellen wasn't stupid. They were probably hoping for this the whole time.

"Well, why don't we discuss that if and when your situation improves?"

Ellen seethed. "My *situation* is just fine. I don't know why you can't understand that I'm not willingly taking time off. It's an *official* request...by the police. I'm not quitting if that's what you're getting at."

Rick had the nerve to sigh. "Let's table this discussion for now and you can let us know when things change."

Ellen couldn't believe this. "I want some kind of guarantee that I can come back to my job, Rick."

Rick had the nerve to look sympathetic. "Until you know how long you're going to be out, there's no way we can make any guarantees. As it is we'll at least have to bring in a temp and eventually a replacement if you're going to be gone for a considerable amount of time."

"A replacement?" Ellen was perilously close to shrieking. "I just told you I'm not quitting. I'm coming back. You can't just replace me. This is my job. You can't do this to me."

She stared at Rick, who had turned an alarming shade of red, and felt a measure of satisfaction that she'd pushed back as hard as he was pushing her. Then the other chick stood up and Ellen steeled herself to battle this one as well.

"I'm going to ask you to lower your voice," she said, her own voice low and calm.

Ellen had no intentions of doing anything this woman said. "WHO ARE YOU TO TELL ME WHAT TO DO?"

Rick stood up and placed himself between them. "Ellen, Diane's the administrative vice president. She's in charge of all of the staff."

"SO?" Ellen was in full rage now. "DID YOU TELL HER ABOUT ME? DID YOU TELL HER I SAVED YOUR ASS? DID YOU?"

"I know all about you, Ellen," the Diane chick said, her voice still low and calm. "And I think under the circumstances you would be better off taking care of your family."

Ellen fought to control her anger. "And what about my job? What about when I come back?"

"Consider your leave permanent," she answered. "We'll be making other arrangements as far as staffing is concerned."

"So you're firing me," Ellen stated flatly, and both of the assholes in front of her nodded. "You know you have to have a reason to fire me. You can't fire people just because you feel like it."

The woman gave her a level look. "We have sufficient evidence to support your separation, Mrs. Shepherd," she said, and Ellen knew it was true. She knew that they had been trying to fire her from day one. Rick probably had a whole file cabinet full of grievances against her.

Rather than give them the satisfaction of knowing how much they upset her, Ellen turned and walked out.

Since she'd never had a permanent place in the office, there wasn't anything for her to pick up so, without a word to anyone, Ellen simply walked out the front door.

"Any problems?" Frank asked her.

Ellen shook her head. "No, they were sorry to see me go, but they said they understand," she answered.

FOURTEEN

Krissy

It was almost worse having her mother around all the time. Krissy knew it was too much to hope that her mother would be happy to be home with them, but it hurt to see how little she cared to interact with them.

The first few days, James and Krissy would sit at the table, anticipating a hot breakfast, while their mother sat staring at nothing over a cooling cup of coffee. Both were too afraid to ask their mother for something to eat and eventually settled on whatever they could find in the pantry. By the end of that first week, they were automatically pulling out their own bowls and fixing their own cold cereal, then cleaning up after their meal.

Under her mother's baleful eye, Krissy didn't know what to do with herself other than stay out of her mother's way. James seemed to feel the same and avoided the first floor altogether, opting for self-confinement in his room. Unfortunately, it was sweltering hot, and Krissy felt like the house was baking her as she sat and stared out at the fields in front of her. Even with her bedroom windows opened wide, the air hung still and thick with searing sunlight and humidity.

She barely stirred when James let himself in and closed the door behind him. Bypassing the bed, he lay out flat on the bare wood of the floor as if it had the power to magically conduct the heat away from his body. Krissy watched him close his eyes and only vaguely wondered why he had come in. But languor took over and she let her eyelids droop until her sweat glued them shut.

Ellen

God, it was hot. Ellen swiped at the bead of sweat that ran down along her hairline, tickling the fine hairs that grew there. It felt too much like a bug crawling on her, which only added to the seething anger that lay festering in the pit of her stomach. If it weren't for those stupid kids she'd be sitting in the cool air-conditioning of the hospital right now and not melting in this crap house she'd been forced to move to.

Ellen could feel her resentment spreading through her like a virus. How could she have been so stupid marrying someone so far beneath her? Of course all of her girlfriends had raved about Frank, how he was *sooo* nice and *sooo* handsome and look what a good job he did taking care of his mother before she died and blah blah blah. God, she had been a moron to listen to them. And where were they all now? Huh? They all got to live in nice homes in Springfield and she was stuck way out in the sticks like some farmer's wife. Except her farmer didn't even have a goddamn farm. Instead he had a tiny little farmhouse on a tiny little postage stamp that he didn't even own.

What a joke. Her whole life was one big joke. And if there was one thing Ellen knew she didn't appreciate one bit, it was humor.

FIFTEEN

Krissy

Krissy had been dozing against the window when the sound of a massive carpenter bee tapping on her screen woke her up. She sat up and idly swatted it away, then realized it was on the outside of her screen. Still bleary, she glanced at her clock and saw that it was well into the afternoon, and their mother hadn't called them down for lunch. It didn't really matter, anyway. It was too hot to eat.

Krissy saw James fast asleep on her floor and considered waking him for a moment but let the moment pass. Instead, she turned back to the window and watched the bee butt its furry head against her screen. She reached out to touch it as it landed. Just past the end of her finger, she spied a dark figure move through the corn in front of their house. Krissy quickly pulled her hand from the screen, startling the bee into flight.

"James," Krissy whispered, keeping her eyes on the form that had paused just inside the row closest to their driveway. "James."

"Whu...?" James replied and then sat up and rubbed at his eyes.

"Come here," she whispered and shifted to the side of the dormer so whoever it was who was watching their house wouldn't see her.

To make her point, Krissy pointed out the window and opened her eyes wide.

James moved over and stood behind her, his eyes following the direction of her finger.

"Who is that?" he whispered. Krissy could tell he was fully awake.

"I don't know," she answered. "He just showed up."

James and Krissy held still and watched the shadow watching them. Krissy held her breath for what seemed like forever and then startled when the figure moved through the corn and onto their driveway.

He was older than they were, and the first thing Krissy noticed was that he looked a lot like Zach but as if someone had put his face together wrong. He had the same black hair and Krissy would bet good money he had the same dark eyes, but where Zach was tan and fit from years of farm work, the kid in front of them was pale and soft with fat clumping around his middle like a poorly tucked-in shirt.

Krissy and James watched him slowly cross their driveway, his eyes on their house the entire time. He seemed to be watching the front door, not realizing that he was being observed from the second-floor window. Krissy knew their house looked more like a one story. She knew a girl from school who lived in a house just like theirs, but there was no second story, and the dormer windows along the roof were fake.

By the time he reached the edge of their front yard, Krissy could see that he looked almost exactly like Zach. He had the same dark eyes, though his were set in a face pale and round and dotted with acne. She noticed a bit of stubble along his chin and realized he was older than she originally thought, like maybe more than twenty.

Krissy and James watched silently, barely breathing as the watcher paused just inside their yard and then turned and made his way around the corner of the house. Without a word they flew across the room and opened the door. James stopped Krissy for a moment and listened. They could hear the TV on downstairs, so they braved the hallway and entered James's room across the hall. They made it to the window in time to see the man pause and peer into the kitchen window, then make his way over to the window that looked into Grandma Naomi's room. Krissy knew he wouldn't be able to see anything. Grandma Naomi often suffered terrible headaches and their father had hung blackout curtains on all her windows.

They lost sight of him as he made his way around the other end of the house, but they didn't dare go into their parents' room. Instead, they rushed back to Krissy's room and waited. It wasn't long before he appeared around the opposite corner and stopped near the living room window. Krissy could hear him listening to the TV and wondered why her mother didn't see him standing there. The living room curtains were thin and easy to see through. She only had to look to the right and she would have seen him easily.

Krissy wondered if she should tell her mother someone was in their yard, but by the time she'd worked it out in her head, the man turned and made his way back across the driveway and into the corn. Krissy and James watched as the black dot of his hair waded through the cornstalks and then released the breath they had been holding when he disappeared.

"Who do you think that was?" Krissy asked as she rubbed at her arms. Goosebumps had risen all over her and she shivered despite the heat.

"I don't know," James answered, looking as freaked out as Krissy felt. "He looks a lot like Zach. Maybe that's Mr. Harper's other son... Jeremy."

"Why do you think he was here?"

James shrugged. "Zach's come to check on us a couple of times. Maybe he or Mr. Harper sent him here to see if we were OK."

"Then why didn't he knock on the door?" Krissy asked but didn't really expect an answer.

James shrugged again. He didn't really have an answer for that.

Ellen

As Ellen dozed on the couch, she had no idea she was being observed. It wasn't until the TV blared a commercial for The Ellen DeGeneres Show that her namesake woke up groggy and aching from the awkward position in which she had slept. Ellen sat up and rubbed at her neck and idly watched the previews for that afternoon's episode. She always found it ironic that the women in her community all claimed that homosexuality was immoral and staunchly denied gays the right to marry but fell all over themselves at the awesomeness that was Ellen DeGeneres. It boggled the mind. Ellen Shepherd couldn't care less about the other Ellen other than to silently offer her a "good fucking job" for proving that all of conservative America was a fat bunch of hypocrites.

Ohio Ellen stood and stretched and then walked into the kitchen, never realizing someone was staring at her through the wide expanse of her living room window.

SIXTEEN

Krissy

Krissy stared out across the cornfield waiting for the black dot to reemerge on the other side. James sat down on the bench next to her and waited as well. It wasn't long before they saw the man appear in the distance and make his way across Mr. Harper's farm and enter one of the barns.

"He must be Mr. Harper's son," Krissy said quietly as if the man still stood outside her window. "He's never been here before. Maybe he didn't realize our house was here."

James shook his head. "It's not like he was here by accident," he intoned gravely. Krissy looked at James, who was sounding older and more serious, like the man Krissy would be proud to call her brother. "He had to have a reason to be here."

Krissy wanted to ask what that reason could be and then realized she was terrified of the answer.

"I'm hungry," James announced, sounding more like her twelve-year-old brother again. "Let's get something to eat."

Krissy followed her brother downstairs and found their mother searching through the refrigerator, muttering curses under her breath.

"There's not a goddamn thing to eat in this house," she complained. Ellen slammed the fridge and stared at her children for one long minute. Krissy fidgeted under her scrutiny, but James stood and returned the stare defiantly.

"Do you two think you can manage to stay inside and not go missing long enough for me to go to the store?" their mother asked.

More than anything, Krissy didn't want her mother leaving the house, but she was too afraid to say so. She knew it would be too much to ask that her mother take them with her.

"We'll be fine," James answered, though Krissy knew it wasn't true.

"There was someone looking at the house earlier," she blurted, then winced under her brother's glare. "He was looking in the windows."

Krissy was happy to see that her mother looked concerned for once.

"What did he look like?" she asked, though it sounded more like a demand.

"He looked like Zach, only fatter," James said reluctantly, still shooting his sister dirty looks.

All the tension seemed to leak out of their mother's body. "That's just Jeremy," she answered, then pulled open the pantry door. "Mr. Harper's son. He has a thing about looking in people's windows. It doesn't mean anything. He probably went back home to mas...mess around with himself."

Krissy wondered what that meant. James gave her a look and shook his head slightly as their mother slammed the door to the pantry.

"Well, can you?" she asked, startling James with her question.

"Can we what?"

"Stay put. I need to get us something for dinner."

James nodded and Krissy followed suit.

"Fine," Ellen said, then grabbed her purse. "I'll be back in a few minutes."

Krissy and James watched their mother stalk out of the house, letting the screen door slam behind her.

"Do you think she'll only be gone a few minutes?" Krissy asked. James snorted but didn't answer.

Ellen

Ellen didn't give Jeremy Harper another thought other than to wonder what took him so long to find their house. He'd been a Peeping Tom for forever and Ellen knew she was an extremely attractive woman. Far more attractive than that girl Heather he'd been busted trying to look at.

Ellen slowed her car near the KFC, but the smell alone was enough to send her off to the grocery store. All that grease was disgusting and Ellen knew if they kept eating fast food she'd be a complete cow in no time.

Even though there was a Kroger just across I-70, it wasn't one she cared to frequent, populated as it was by the lesser mortals of Springfield and parts south. Ellen preferred the one on North Bechtle where the normal people shopped. So what if it was a little farther?

Ellen took the highway and ended up near the mall. Instead of going right toward the nicer Kroger, she went left and pulled into a space outside of JC Penney. Dinner wasn't for another two, three hours, so she had plenty of time to treat herself to some retail therapy.

SEVENTEEN

Krissy

Krissy and James stayed glued to her window, watching the farm in the distance. It was far enough away that they couldn't really see anything more than shapes moving back and forth between buildings. Krissy could distinguish Mr. Harper from the other two men only because he was shorter and much heavier, but Zach and Jeremy looked alike. It seemed like Jeremy was returning to the day-to-day business of running the farm as if his visit to the Shepherd house had never happened. Maybe he really was only checking on them and figured they were OK when he saw their mother in the living room.

James's expression told her he thought otherwise, but he didn't voice his opinion and that was OK with Krissy.

They were so caught up in watching the little that was going on outside, they startled when both their cell phones went off simultaneously. It was a text from their dad making sure they were at home and safe. James returned the text, and without asking, Krissy knew he just confirmed their presence at home and didn't write anything about Jeremy Harper coming to the house or their mother leaving. They resumed their watch of the farm next door, their eyes following the black dots as they moved back and forth across the landscape. But the monotony got the best of them and soon both were fast asleep.

Then their father came home. Early.

Krissy didn't hear him come up the drive, and she was still asleep when he moved through the house, calling out for his wife and then his children. It wasn't until her bedroom door flew open that she and James bolted awake and stared at their father in surprise.

"Jesus Christ," their father panted, and Krissy could see terror draining from their father's face. He didn't come over and hug them or rain kisses on their faces, but that was OK. Krissy could tell from the fear that had tightened the skin around his eyes that he was afraid for them, and that meant that he loved them.

"Where's your mother?" he asked, not even trying to keep his fury out of his voice.

"She said there wasn't anything to eat so she went to the grocery store," James answered.

Frank tried to rub the stress out of his face, and Krissy bet if she pressed her ear to his chest his heart would be going a mile a minute.

"How long has she been gone?"

James glanced at the clock. "Since two."

It was four o'clock. Even Krissy knew it didn't take two hours to make a run to Kroger or even Aldi to pick up dinner. Thinking about dinner made Krissy's tummy rumble loud enough for James and her father to hear.

"Come on," their father said. "I'll make you something to eat."

Downstairs in the kitchen, where their mother wasn't able to find a single thing, Frank Shepherd made tomato soup and grilled cheese sandwiches from ingredients that had magically appeared in the pantry.

They were almost done eating when their mother appeared in the doorway. Krissy couldn't help but notice that she only had a couple of grocery bags. She also looked annoyed for some reason, like her husband was creating a major inconvenience by coming home earlier than usual. Ellen glared at the table.

"Well, that's just great, Frank," she snapped. "Go ahead and ruin their appetite when I had dinner planned already."

"Where were you, Ellen?" Krissy heard her father ask. She didn't want to look at him. There was something in his tone she'd never heard before, a level of anger that transcended rage. Instead she kept her face down, almost touching her plate. She could see out of the corner of her eye that James braved his father's wrath and was watching, open-mouthed at the storm that was brewing in their small kitchen.

Krissy's mother didn't seem to notice that she was straying perilously close to her husband's breaking point.

"At the grocery store, *obviously*," she snapped. "I don't suppose you made enough for everyone, not that I want grilled cheese for dinner."

Frank stared at his wife and then seemed to remember his children. "Go watch some TV," he ordered, then held in his anger until James and Krissy had left the room. James turned on the television but didn't pay attention to the fact that it was turned to the news. Krissy turned and stared at the television while James listened to their parents yelling in the kitchen.

"Since when does it take three hours to buy...spaghetti sauce and ground beef?"

There was a picture of Mason on the screen next to the pretty news anchor, but Krissy couldn't hear what she was saying over her parents' shouting.

"Are you serious? First, who says I was gone three hours, and second, you have no idea how long it takes to buy groceries since *you never do it.*"

Krissy stared as Justice's picture appeared next to Mason's. The pretty anchor looked concerned and Krissy thought that it was really nice of her to worry about someone she didn't even know. The screen changed to another reporter who looked serious, though Krissy still couldn't tell what they were saying. Clinton's picture popped up on the screen next.

"James?" she said quietly, staring at the screen, but her brother was distracted by their parents' fight.

"Do you have *any* idea what's going on?" Frank asked. "Or are you so selfish that you can't even see the danger your own children are in?"

"James?" Krissy said again quietly, staring at the TV.

"What?" James answered without looking.

"Selfish?" her mother shouted. "You're calling *me* selfish? When I'm the one who quit her job to stay home and look after two children who are perfectly capable of looking after themselves? Who lives in this tiny-ass, crappy house that we don't even own when everyone else I know lives in nice homes in actual neighborhoods like normal people? Or how about the fact that I have to put up with a husband who doesn't appreciate a single thing I do who gets to go off to his loser job for twelve hours a day and hang out with his buddies? And I'm the selfish one?"

"James," Krissy said quietly. It was no longer a question. Tears burned her eyes, making the screen in front of her blurry. This time she was glad the sound was turned down.

"What..." James answered, finally turning to see what Krissy was looking at.

Another picture had popped up next to Clinton's. Even through her tears she could see who it was. Minor Allen had disappeared. And from the video it looked like he had been taken from his own front yard.

Ellen

Done. Just done. It was one thing to be living a life much less than she had anticipated, but it was quite another to be treated like some loser, unpaid babysitter. Not only had Frank had the nerve to question her about why she took so long at the grocery store, he even went out and searched her car. It didn't take him long to find the JC Penney and Bon Worth bags in her trunk. It's not like she'd bought a lot, and all of it was on clearance. What really set him off was the Kohl's bags she'd stashed behind the back seats. Maybe there were a few too many, but she needed something to wear now that she was going to be home all the time. Most of her clothes were work outfits, and she couldn't very well sit around the house in a suit. And so what if she'd picked up some things for her mother and brother? They were on sale and she had tons of Kohl's cash to use.

Frank was the most unreasonable husband ever. Ellen seethed over the fact that he'd insisted she return everything she bought and then, when she refused, took the bags and left to do it himself.

Ellen reached for the phone, which rang under her hand, startling her. She wasn't interested in talking to anyone other than her mother. So what if Minor had gone missing? What was she supposed to do about it? Ellen picked up the handset, hung up on whoever was calling, and then picked it up again to call her mother.

EIGHTEEN

Krissy

Krissy sobbed into her pillow while James sat on her window seat and stared off at nothing. She could hear her mother ranting to someone on the phone and knew her father had left to return all the junk her mother had bought when she was supposed to be buying groceries. Her father's absence terrified her. She knew that if the kidnapper walked in right at that moment, her mother would just hand them over with a thank you for stopping by. By the time her father returned, she was too tired to cry anymore but too scared to let herself fall asleep. James seemed to be having the same trouble. He hadn't said a word the entire time but just stared out at the dark, his own tears cutting trails down his cheeks.

Krissy knew Minor's kidnapping was especially hard for James. Though he had grown up with all of the missing boys, he'd known Minor since kindergarten and had shared every class and after-school activity with him for the last eight years. If James played T-ball, Minor played T-ball. If James went to Boy Scout Camp, Minor went to Boy Scout Camp. They essentially lived the same life but from different houses. But Krissy knew, where Justice and Clinton and even Mason were tough boys who could probably withstand the fear and trauma of a kidnapping, Minor was different. It's not that he was weak or sickly or anything. He was just the kind of kid who everyone else took care of, the one who everyone else looked out for. James had been dragging him along since kindergarten, and Krissy knew James was feeling his loss keenly. Krissy had once envied her brother's friendship with Minor, but now, seeing how much James was suffering, she thought that maybe it wasn't such a great thing to be so attached to someone. Maybe her mother had it right, not caring about other people so much.

Krissy curled up on her side and closed her eyes. She wasn't surprised when James crawled in next to her. She listened to his quiet sobs lessen and then disappear. It wasn't until his breathing slowed that Krissy let herself fall asleep.

Ellen

The next morning, Ellen waited until Frank left for work. She usually slept until after he left anyway, so it wasn't hard to pretend to snore while he got dressed. Of course he didn't kiss her good-bye, and she didn't really expect it, though it still made her angry. As soon as the door slammed, Ellen jumped up and pulled her suitcase out of the closet. She waited until she heard his car pull off down the driveway to turn on the bedroom light. As she pulled clothes out of the closet, her anger flamed anew at the insult of having all of her nice new clothes returned without her consent. She filled one suitcase with all her crappy old clothes and then pulled Frank's suitcase out of the closet. It wasn't like he was ever going to need it.

Ellen shoved the last of her things into his bag and sat on it to zip it shut. It weighed a ton, but who cared? She was leaving and that was that.

She'd worn a sweat suit to bed so she wouldn't need to waste time changing. It was already a million degrees in their tiny house and she was regretting her choice of outfit. Oh well, she could change out of it as soon as she got to her mother's house.

Ellen dragged her suitcases down the stairs, trying to be as quiet as possible. She stopped at the bottom and listened, hoping Krissy and James hadn't heard her noisy descent. She really didn't need any drama right now.

Satisfied they had slept through all the noise and commotion, Ellen stepped into the kitchen and dropped the note she'd written to Frank on the table. It had taken her hours, but it was all worth it to let him know exactly what a disappointment he and the life he'd given her had been.

With as much quiet as she could manage, Ellen opened the door, pulled her bags out behind her, then pulled them over and loaded them into her car. In the dark she didn't notice the figure standing just inside the corn, staring at her.

NINETEEN

Krissy

Krissy was sitting at the kitchen table, staring at her mother's note, when James walked in.

"What is that?" he asked.

"A note for Dad," she answered quietly.

"From who?"

"From Mom."

James's face went still. He moved over and sat at the seat next to her. The note lay in front of them, several pages of paper covered with handwriting. Though their mother had folded it, the pages had refused to stay closed and the note had opened like the petals of the flower looking for sunlight.

"What does it say?" James asked.

Krissy looked at her brother sadly. "She left us."

James looked surprised. "That's what it says?"

Krissy shook her head. "I didn't read it. I saw it and then went upstairs and looked in her room. All her clothes are gone."

James's mouth turned down at the corners. "Maybe we should read the note."

"It's for Dad," Krissy said again.

Krissy and James sat in silence and stared at the note for a long time.

Ellen

Ellen's mother was less than thrilled to see her so early in the morning but let her in with only a little bit of grumbling. Ellen was surprised to see her brother Jerry up and sitting at the kitchen table, twitching like something was stinging him when nothing was there. Ellen wondered if they'd bothered to give him medication for whatever was wrong with him.

"We got up early to make sure you could get in," her mother said with less grace than Ellen had expected. "I guess you'll want to stay in your old room."

Ellen nodded and then stood and waited for her mother to escort her to the back of the house. Instead she just stood there and stared at Ellen.

"Well, you know where it is. You can stay tonight, but you'll have to find your own place tomorrow. I'm going back to bed."

Ellen stared at her mother's retreating back and then turned and looked at her brother, who was mumbling at the table as if he was in deep conversation with his placemat.

Ellen sighed and pulled her luggage into her old room and slammed the door.

TWENTY

Krissy

It occurred to Krissy that they should call their father to tell him about the note, but no sooner had the thought crossed her mind when James's phone went off. James scrambled to answer it.

"Dad?" he said, his voice cracking with stress. Krissy could barely hear her father, but he sounded upset.

"No, she's not here," James answered. "There's a note on the table for you."

James listened again then shook his head. "No...I can't read it to you. It's really long anyway."

Krissy shook her head slowly. She really didn't want to know what was in the note either. There were probably grown-up things in there that really weren't their business. It kind of scared her to think what their mother had written about them.

"OK," James replied and hung up. "Dad's going to try to come home early again."

Krissy nodded and realized they were home alone. The idea terrified her. She turned and looked at the back door and saw that her mother hadn't locked it when she left. James followed her look, jumped up and turned the bolt, and then ran to the front door to check that it was bolted as well. When they returned to the kitchen, James sat as Krissy pulled out cereal and milk for breakfast. They ate quickly, and Krissy put their bowls in the sink.

"We should go upstairs and watch for Dad," James said.

Krissy nodded and the two ran up to Krissy's room and slammed the door behind them. For added measure, James pulled Krissy's desk in front of the door and then joined her on the window seat. No one was moving around at the Harper's, and from her window, Krissy couldn't see anyone near their own houseeither. Way off to the left where the old Shepherd barns stood, they could see someone walking back and forth, but it too far to tell who it was.

If they lived in the old house, though, it would have been a different situation.

Before Krissy or James or even their father came into the world, the Shepherd family lived in the original farmhouse at the back of the property. It was much larger and much older than the house they lived in now. When Grandpa Nate married the woman who would eventually give birth to their father, his pa gave him a small plot closer to the road to build his own house. Then family just started dying. First Krissy's Great Grandmother Agatha died of influenza, then her children from various illnesses and accidents. Then Great Grandpa Frank had a massive heart attack and joined his wife and children in the cemetery. Grandpa Nate had planned to move his family back to the big house, but just before the move, a freak bolt of lightning burned it to the ground. Luckily, Grandpa Nate's little house was far enough away that it was spared, though the crops around the main house weren't so lucky. Only an old barn and a decrepit shed were left. Eventually Mr. Harper bought everything from Grandpa

Nate, and Krissy suspected that the reason why her grandfather didn't just give this house to his son was because he didn't actually own it. The thought that their only home was a borrowed house was really depressing, and in a way, Krissy didn't blame her mother for not wanting to stay.

Krissy watched the movement around the old barn while James kept a lookout for their father. Eventually boredom took over, and despite her earlier terror, Krissy's eyes began to droop. Before she could fall asleep, James startled her awake.

"Dad's here," he said with relief, then jumped up. James pushed the desk aside and opened the door for their dad, who stepped in and in an uncharacteristic move, knelt down and pulled them into his arms. Krissy closed her eyes and sank into his embrace. She could feel a sob building in her chest and fought to hold it in until James pulled his arm out and put it around her. She could tell he was trying to be brave, so she let go for him and began to cry.

"I'm so sorry," her dad whispered. "I tried to get away as fast as I could."

Krissy felt her father let go and quickly wiped her eyes on her T-shirt. She tried not to notice when James did the same and instead looked at her father. He'd aged in the hours since she saw him last, and Krissy worried about him worrying about them.

"We're going to go get your mom back, OK?" he said with an earnestness that Krissy didn't share.

James shook his head.

"She won't come back," he said. Krissy could hear both anger and sadness in his voice.

"Sure she will, bud," Frank replied. "We just need to let her know how important it is."

James shook his head again. "That won't matter to her. She said in her note that she never wanted this kind of life in the first place. She doesn't want to be with any of us anymore."

Krissy stared at her brother. She didn't realize he'd read the note. She wondered what the rest of it said and then realized it didn't matter. Krissy reached up and rubbed at the pain in her chest. Her heart hurt deep inside of her, and more than anything she wanted to cry again. It wasn't that she thought James or her father would think less of her if she let the tears that were burning her eyes actually fall. She just didn't want to cry anymore over someone who wouldn't cry for her. She could tell that James felt the same. His eyes stared, hot and shining, but his cheeks were dry, and Krissy knew her expression mirrored his.

Their father looked at them with sadness.

"I'm sorry," he said simply. "I know I failed you guys. I couldn't get her to understand...that you needed her. I let you down and I'm sorry."

Krissy gave her father another hug and felt the hurt in her heart lessen as his arms held her tight. Both were smiling, albeit sadly, when she pulled away.

"Well, we can at least try and get her to come home," he said with false enthusiasm. Krissy and James played along and smiled.

Ellen

Ellen wasn't having very much luck. Jobs were few and far between in Springfield and landlords weren't willing to take a chance on a renter who wasn't employed. She finally found a crap attic apartment near the local university that smelled of mold and cat pee and was so small she could traverse its entire length in two seconds. The previous tenant had left a faded, smelly futon and a card table with a single chair, which the landlord joked meant the apartment was rented "furnished." Ellen stared at both with distaste but demurred when the landlord asked if she wanted them removed. She didn't have the money for furniture after paying the security deposit and first month's rent.

Once she inspected the closet she'd just rented, Ellen locked up and set off in search of employment.

By the end of the day, Ellen's mood was sour. She'd applied everywhere only to be told they weren't looking for anyone, even though most of the businesses she'd gone to had employment ads in the paper. By the time she'd hit the mall and most of the stores she frequented, Ellen was furious. She'd spent enough money there that you'd think the least they could do was consider her for a job there. Even Kohl's had the nerve to turn her down, and most of the people who worked there were losers.

Ellen stopped into Kroger to pick up something for dinner and, in a fit of pique, filled out an application. To her horror the manager hired her on the spot. More than anything she wanted to tell that fat bastard what he could do with his shitty job, but for once, Ellen kept her mouth shut and reluctantly agreed to start the next day.

She left Kroger with her new uniform and drove the distance to her mother's house to pick up her suitcases.

It irritated her that her mother insisted she ring the doorbell like a guest. Her clothes were in the room she'd grown up in. Why should she have to stand there like a stranger waiting for someone to open the goddamn door? And why was it taking so long?

Ellen held the bell down and glared at the door in front of her. The sound of the bell clanging on the other side gave her little satisfaction and the sight of her idiot brother gave her even less. Jerry looked like he'd been sleeping and it angered her that he could sit around doing his twitchy disabled thing while she was forced to beg for a job and a place to stay like some kind of loser. And she was pretty sure she bought those clothes he was wearing. Well if her mother expected Ellen to cough up any more money she had another thing coming. Ellen was going to need every dime to pay for that apartment.

Ellen pushed past her brother and shivered. The house was freezing cold despite the heat of the day. It did nothing to cool her off, though, as her mother stepped out of her bedroom bleary-eyed and disheveled. She couldn't believe that while she was out trying to find a job and a place to live, her mother and brother were lazing about like they didn't have a care in the world.

"I see you found something," her mother said, then nodded at the royal blue polo shirt Ellen had brought in for some reason.

"Yeah, well, it's just temporary until I can find something more suited to my skill set," Ellen snapped.

"Well, that's good," her mother yawned. "My car payment is due soon and you haven't given me a check yet."

Ellen stared at her mother. Was she serious?

"I just spent the last of my savings on a shithole apartment that you told me I had to get," Ellen said.

"You got a job, too," her mother countered.

Ellen shook her head in disbelief. "So? You think they started paying me the minute I walked in the door?"

"You have to have something, Ellen," her mother insisted. "I need to make the payment tomorrow."

Was she serious? Ellen couldn't wrap her head around it. "I don't have it, Mom. I don't know what to tell you."

Ellen watched her mother's face turn stony and cold. "Maybe you should have thought of us before you ran off and left a perfectly good situation," she snapped, then turned back into her bedroom and slammed the door.

Ellen turned and looked at her brother, who gave her his own glare, followed his mother's suit, and took refuge in his own bedroom.

Alone in the hallway, Ellen considered knocking on the door and apologizing. It was something she did a lot as a child. But she knew it would only invite more anger and acrimony from her mother, which would be made much worse by the fact that Ellen did not have a single dime to make her mother's car payment. She couldn't even use one of her credit cards, since all of those were maxed out as well.

With as much quiet as possible, Ellen pulled her two suitcases down the hall and out of the house, then drove back to the hovel she now called home. Once she'd put everything away and given the space a cursory cleaning, she sat down on the smelly futon and stared at nothing.

For all the debt and suffering she had endured on behalf of her family, Ellen realized she was left with little. Her husband had practically run her out of the house, forcing her to leave behind her own children; her boss had manipulated her into quitting; and her own mother had spent her into the poorhouse. Now all she had was a crap job and an even crappier apartment while they all profited off her misery.

Ellen lay down and pressed her burning head against the cool of the sheets she'd bought to cover the offensive mattress. She could still smell the acrid stench of piss. It made her eyes burn and tear, validating the suffering she was forced to endure.

TWENTY ONE

Krissy

Their trip to retrieve their mother had ended in failure. Not only was her mother not at her grandmother's house, Grandma Wermer had no idea where her own daughter could be. All she could tell them was that Krissy's mother had taken a job at one of the Kroger stores in town, and she thought maybe she'd rented an apartment nearby. Since she didn't know which Kroger her mother was working at, there was no way to know where the apartment could be.

Krissy knew from her father's expression that he was angry with her grandmother. His anger was made worse when Grandma Wermer complained that her car payment was due and hinted that since her daughter couldn't pay it, Frank was somehow responsible. Krissy gave her dad a lot of credit. Instead of yelling at his mother-in-law, he simply walked away.

There were only three Kroger stores in Springfield, and Ellen wasn't at any of them. For all they knew, Grandma Wermer had told them the wrong store and they were looking in all the wrong places. Krissy thought for sure Grandma Wermer was wrong. There was no way her mother would agree to work in a grocery store. Krissy thought it was more likely she found a job at the mall or in a doctor's office. Her father seemed to think so, too, when he pulled up in front of JC Penney.

The mall was small and it didn't take them long to determine that Ellen wasn't there, either.

Rather than spend the day driving in circles looking for his wife, Frank just drove home. Krissy was glad. She was tired and a little carsick from all the driving around. Her head hurt from unshed tears, and all she really wanted to do was lie down for a little while. As her father slowed to a stop in front of the house, she was surprised to see Zach sitting on their front steps. He stood and smiled as they all got out. Krissy stepped forward with her father while James hung back.

"Hey," he called over, and Krissy watched her dad step up and shake Zach's hand. "My uncle sent me over to make sure everything was OK," he said. "We saw Mrs. Shepherd's car leave just after yours and he was worried these two were home alone again."

"Their mother had a family emergency," she heard her father say, then wondered why he was lying. "I have the rest of the day off, but I'll have to find someone to stay with them during the day until we get our family situation worked out."

Zach nodded. "We wondered if it was something like that. Well Aunt Patty told me to bring them over if you needed someplace for them to go. She's not doing much right now, so she said she'd be happy to keep an eye on them."

Krissy looked up at her dad, who seemed to be considering this. In the car he had said he was going to ask Mrs. Guthrie to watch them, but this was much better. The Harpers were right next door, and with four adults on the farm, there was no way anything bad could happen to them. Frank seemed to agree and thanked Zach.

"I don't want to cut through the field. We'll just drive over to thank Tom and Pat," he said.

Zach laughed. "No problem, but I'm going to take the shortcut," he joked, then disappeared through the corn.

Krissy and James got back into the car and settled in for the short drive to the Harper's house. Krissy glanced at her brother, who sat staring pensively out the window.

"What?" she asked, but he only shook his head in answer.

Krissy looked out the window as her father slowed to a stop in the Harper's yard. Mrs. Harper had come out of the house and stood waiting on their porch, while Mr. Harper stepped out of the barn in the distance with Jeremy behind him. Jeremy paused in the doorway of the barn, and Krissy watched him watching his father cross the wide farm yard to where her father stood. Unless their father told them otherwise, Krissy and James stayed put in the backseat of the car.

"Why do you look so mad?" Krissy asked, keeping her voice low.

James shook his head again, but this time he answered. "I don't think we should be staying here...not after Jeremy Harper tried looking into our house."

"But he was just checking up on us," Krissy protested. "It's like Zach said. They can see everything that goes on at our house and they're worried about us."

James shrugged but didn't answer. Krissy could tell he wasn't convinced. She wanted to continue the debate, but just then her father waved them over. Krissy opened the door and stepped out with her brother right behind her.

"Kids, this is Miss Pat," her father said. Krissy was happy to see how relieved he looked. "She's going to look after you while I'm at work." Krissy's father turned back to Mrs. Harper. "I'll see if I can't adjust my hours so that I'm not leaving so early. I don't want to impose on you any more than I already am. Hopefully I can convince their mother to come back."

Mrs. Harper gave them a slow smile. "It's no problem," she said slowly. Krissy wondered if there was something wrong with Mrs. Harper. She sounded like one of the patients at Spring Haven. "We'll be just fine, won't we kids?"

Krissy nodded politely and wondered if James maybe had a point. Mrs. Harper seemed awfully out of it to be a good babysitter.

Their dad offered his thanks again, and the Shepherd family got into the car and drove back home.

With their dad home, James and Krissy relaxed in front of the television while he called his work. The events of the day finally caught up with Krissy, and she soon fell asleep.

Ellen

Ellen stared at the ancient cashier slowly explaining the intricacies of pushing buttons and couldn't believe how far she'd fallen. She was standing there in an ill-fitting, hideously colored polo shirt learning a job a monkey could do. Why did they even need cashiers when they had a perfectly good self-checkout?

Ellen nodded absently, then turned and looked longingly at the front door in the hopes that Frank would appear and beg her to come home. Even better if he were standing there begging her holding all the bags of clothes he'd forced her to return. The elderly cashier broke through her reverie.

"Yes, I get it," Ellen snapped, then moved the woman aside and took her place at the register. She bristled when the other woman had the nerve to supervise her first few transactions like Ellen had no clue what she was doing. Anyone could wave food over a scanner and hit total. Finally the woman seemed satisfied and wandered off. Ellen felt less than gracious as her line began to back up. Apparently everyone got the memo that Ellen was the only person ringing people up despite the fact that the other cashiers were just standing around chatting. It figures that Ellen would be doing everyone's job...again.

By the time her shift was over, Ellen's spark of anger had turned cold. Frank hadn't shown up to rescue her nor had her mother come to support her. The only person to show her any encouragement was the morbidly obese manager, who came over twice to tell Ellen what a great job she was doing and shove his disgusting belly in her direction. She knew what he wanted, and she wasn't about to stoop to dating her boss for special favors...at least not yet.

Dispirited, Ellen got in her car and headed for home. It wasn't until the pothole just before Crybaby Bridge jolted her out of her reverie that she realized she was heading for the wrong home. Ellen stopped just in front of the old pumping station and turned around. Out of the corner of her eye, she saw a movement among the trees. She didn't bother to stop and look. It didn't have anything to do with her.

TWENTY TWO

Krissy

Krissy's eyes wouldn't open. She knew her father was shaking her awake, but it was just too early to get up.

"Krissy, honey," she heard her dad say. "Come on, baby. I need you to get up, OK?"

Krissy nodded and, with her eyes still closed, pushed herself off the bed and tried to sit.

"I need to drop you off at the Harper's," her father said quietly. "You can probably go back to sleep there."

Krissy swayed on her bed, her head groggy and still full of sleep. She felt a hand go under her arm and lift her to standing. When she opened her eyes she saw her father pulling clean clothes out of her dresser.

"Here." He handed her a T-shirt and shorts and clean underpants, then left the room. Krissy slowly changed and went into the bathroom to pee and wash her face. She could hear her dad in James's room. A moment later, James emerged and took her place in the bathroom. When he was done, they followed their father down the stairs and out to the car. Krissy was so tired she barely noticed it was still dark outside. She dozed the short distance to the Harper's house and barely woke when her father opened the back door of the car.

"I'm sorry it's so early," she heard her father say. "I'll see if I can't change my hours after today."

She heard someone answer, but she was too tired to make out their words.

"I can't thank you enough for this," he continued, then ushered Krissy and James toward the house.

Krissy moved slowly and followed the dark figure inside, James right behind her. Through bleary eyes she saw the figure disappear down a long dark hallway. She paused, then jumped a bit when James bumped into her. Then a light through an open doorway appeared at the end of the hallway and the figure beckoned her forward. Krissy obeyed and made her way down the hallway to where the light cut across the wood floor. She paused and stepped through the doorway. It was a small bedroom with two small quilt covered beds, a bedside table with a dimly lit lamp between them.

"I know you kids are probably still exhausted," the voice said. It sounded a lot like Mr. Harper and the awake part of Krissy's brain thought that was weird. "You two can lie down in here for a while."

Krissy didn't need to hear anything else and gratefully made her way to the closest bed and sank into it. She had no idea where James was and at that moment, she didn't care. Soon she was fast asleep.

Ellen

Ellen stared out the store's windows, watched the sky slowly turn from black to blue, and knew she'd made a mistake. She could blame

Frank for being mean or stubborn, but the truth was she'd let her pride and anger get the best of her again. Frank wasn't going to show up to beg her to come home. Her mother wasn't going to tearfully admit that she'd taken advantage of Ellen and apologize. And Rick certainly wasn't going to beg her to come back to her cushy job at the medical center. She'd burned all of those bridges and many more, but it wasn't until long after the ashes had settled that she regretted it.

Ellen heard her name and turned. The fat pig of a manager was beckoning her to his office, where she knew he'd lecture her on customer service while surreptitiously massaging the bulge at the front of his pants. She'd only worked three shifts and had already spent half of them in his office. She sighed and then turned to follow him in.

TWENTY THREE

Krissy

Krissy awoke to the sound of dishes crashing. She looked around in confusion at the unfamiliar room. James had awakened too and was just sitting up.

"Dang, I'm still tired," he yawned. Krissy was about to agree when another crash came from outside the door. Then Mrs. Harper appeared in the doorway. She was wearing a silky robe over an old housecoat, and her hair stood up at the back as if she'd just awakened as well.

"I got some cereal out for you kids," she said slowly. "You like cereal, right?"

Krissy and James nodded and followed Mrs. Harper down the hall to the kitchen, where the table was set with several boxes of different types of cereal, milk, and bowls. A broken bowl lay on the counter next to a pile of dirty pots and pans. They looked like they had fallen over, and dirty water cascaded across the counter and onto the floor.

Krissy took a seat at the table with James next to her. Of all the boxes in front of her, only one was kid friendly. Krissy poured herself a bowl of Cheerios and then handed the box to James. They stared into their bowls as Mrs. Harper moved about the kitchen cleaning the mess she'd made. She moved slowly as if every step gave her pain. There was a half-full coffee cup near Krissy that did not smell like coffee. Rather, it smelled thick and sweet, like cough medicine. Mrs. Harper seemed to remember her cup and picked it up from the table to add it to the pile of dishes at the sink. But instead of pouring it out, she drank it until it was empty and then ran it under the hot running water.

When they were finished, Krissy carried their bowls to the sink, where Mrs. Harper took them with a smile.

"Thank you, dear," she said in her slow voice. "Why don't you two go see what's on the television?"

Krissy nodded politely, and then she and James stepped out of the kitchen. Unfortunately, they found themselves in a wide but dark hallway with no idea where to go. Krissy only had a vague memory of walking into the house, so she turned right and walked toward the front door. To the left was an open archway that led to what looked like a living room, and to the right was a dark and dusty dining room that looked like it hadn't been used in months. Though the house was large, and every room had several large windows, it was still strangely dark inside.

Unsure of exactly what they were supposed to do, Krissy and her brother slowly made their way into the living room and sat on the old floral couch. There was an ancient console television in front of them. James looked around but couldn't find a remote anywhere, so they instead they sat quietly and listened to the sound of pots being dropped into the sink.

They were startled when Zach walked in.

"You guys don't want to watch TV?" he asked.

"There's no remote," James answered.

Zach chuckled. "Oh, right. This probably seems like an antique to you." He crossed the living room and pressed a wooden panel, which popped open to reveal a cable box and DVD player. On the shelf next to the cable box was a familiar black remote. Krissy and James had the identical remote at home.

Zach pressed a button on the television and aimed the remote at the cable box. The sound of a game show blared through the room, assaulting Krissy's ears. Zach winced and turned the volume down, then handed the remote to Krissy.

"Here you go," he said with a smile. He turned to James. "If you don't feel like watching television, we could use some help out on the farm."

James shrugged, then got up and followed Zach out the front door. Krissy frowned. Why wouldn't Zach let her help, too?

Krissy stared at the game show, too afraid to change the channel. When the noises in the kitchen stopped, Mrs. Harper came in and sat down next to her, another mug of not-coffee in her hand.

"Oh, you don't want to watch this," she said, taking the remote out of Krissy's hand. Mrs. Harper surfed through the channels and then left it on *Sid the Science Kid* on public television. Krissy frowned but said nothing. Maybe Mrs. Harper didn't know it was a baby show.

After a few minutes, Mrs. Harper asked, "Do you watch this?"

Krissy wanted to be polite, but Sid was starting to get on her nerves so she shook her head.

"Oh...I guess it's a little young for you," Mrs. Harper murmured, then pressed the remote again. This time she landed on some judge show. Krissy had never seen it before, but at least it was kind of interesting.

She glanced over and wasn't surprised to see Mrs. Harper's eyes closed. Krissy turned back to the television.

Krissy was so engrossed in the marathon of daytime programming that she'd lost track of time. She heard the door slam and saw that James had come in with Zach, Jeremy, and Mr. Harper behind him. She moved farther into the corner of the sofa as Mr. Harper walked over and nudged his wife.

"Pat...Pat," he said quietly, but Mrs. Harper was completely out. He gave Krissy an embarrassed smile.

"Why don't you come into the kitchen and I'll get us all some lunch."

Krissy got up and followed him into the kitchen and sat down at the table. James sat down on one side and, to her surprise and delight, Zach sat down on the other.

Zach laid his hand on Krissy's head. "Your hair's so short...you almost look like your brother," he said with a smile. Normally Krissy would be thrilled that Zach noticed her, but instead it made her uncomfortable and a little bit sick. Maybe it was because Jeremy was glaring at her from the doorway, or maybe it was from sleeping during the day, but more than anything, Krissy wanted Zach to take his hand back.

Zach gave the hair just behind her ear a gentle tug and then got up to help his uncle.

After lunch, Zach took James back outside and Krissy returned to the couch.

Krissy sat at the end of the couch and watched sitcom reruns for the rest of the day. Mrs. Harper seemed to rouse just as the front door opened. Krissy was happy to see her father walk in behind Mr. Harper.

"Hey, sweetheart," he said, his expression both concerned and embarrassed. "You ready to go?"

Krissy nodded and got up.

"Oh, of course." Mrs. Harper stood up and swayed for a moment before finding her balance. "We had a lovely time, right, honey?"

"Yes, ma'am," Krissy answered politely. "Thank you."

"No problem." Mrs. Harper seemed more with it after her long nap. "We'll see you tomorrow."

Krissy smiled and followed her father out the door. James was already outside, and after several more gestures of thanks, they left for home.

Krissy was surprised to see her dad turn left out of the Harper's driveway instead of right toward their own driveway.

"Where are we going?" she asked, and her dad turned around and smiled.

"I thought we'd go out for hamburgers." James and Krissy gave each other big smiles. It was the first time in weeks that Krissy felt a stirring of happiness and she could tell James felt the same. She settled into her seat and watched with quiet joy as the scenery changed as they drove into town.

Ellen

She just couldn't do it anymore. That disgusting pig of a manager had crossed the line this time. She still couldn't believe the man had the nerve to rub his erection against her in front of everyone in the store.

Of course no one could tell he had a hard-on, as fat as he was. But Ellen could tell the moment it jabbed her in the ass when he slid behind her at the register to show her how to change the register tape. It was disgusting and humiliating and Ellen was so horrified that she left without even punching out. As she drove away from the store, she was shocked to find tears falling down her face. She'd never cried like this before.

Ellen was so dispirited that she drove past her apartment and all the way through town before she realized she was almost to the home she had abandoned. In an uncharacteristic move, she took it as a sign and pulled into the driveway. The house was dark and Ellen assumed Frank and the kids had gone somewhere for dinner, so she pulled into the covered carport and got out.

With the cloud cover, there was no moonlight to illuminate her path from the carport to the house. Ellen carefully made her way across the small backyard toward the rear of the house. She was not quite to the back door when a dark figure came around the corner of the house and crossed in front of her. Startled, Ellen stopped short.

"Jesus Christ!" she blurted, her hand going to her chest. "You scared the shit out of me." Ellen took a step toward the figure and looked closely, then took a step back in surprise. "What are *you* doing here?" she asked, her tone angry for having been so startled. In the dark the shadow turned as if to move away then turned back quickly and closed the distance between them. Ellen felt fingers tearing into the soft skin of her neck and then the dark night turned black.

The heels of Ellen's cheap tennis shoes carved lines across the hardpan of the backyard. The rough scraping was loud enough to give her killer pause to listen in case someone had overheard them. Then her body was shoved into the trunk of her own car. If Ellen had still been alive she would have felt the rumble of the engine and the lurch of the car as it backed out of the carport and onto the driveway. She would have felt the car bounce from the unevenness of the gravel driveway, then the sudden loss of it as the car moved onto the smooth blacktop of the road. And if she'd been alive she would have been furious to see her car backing into a leaning carport of an abandoned home in the worst neighborhood in Springfield, and embarrassed to admit that her car was just crappy enough to blend in perfectly with its new surroundings. And she would have been shocked to know that this was to be her final resting place as her killer calmly walked away, leaving her hidden in plain sight.

TWENTY FOUR

Krissy

Krissy was full and happy when they pulled up to their house. Even James seemed to be in a better mood, though he still looked distracted. Inside, their father sent them up to get ready for bed. Even though it was a little early, Krissy was tired from getting up so early, and she knew her dad wanted to make some more calls to try to find their mother. So without complaint, Krissy obeyed and wasn't surprised when James followed close behind.

She had just pulled her pajama shirt over her head when James walked into her room, his hair still wet and dripping from his shower. Krissy noted how tired he looked when he fell onto her bed.

"Are you going to sleep early?" she asked, just to have something to ask. James nodded and yawned.

"They had me pulling weeds," he said through another yawn. "I think I pulled a whole field before Mr. Harper told me I could stop."

"It's nice, them letting us stay with them, isn't it?" Krissy said as she sat down cross-legged at the end of her bed.

"Yeah," James answered. "At first it was kind of uncomfortable because that Jeremy guy kept following me everywhere, but Zach told me that Mr. Harper said they were supposed to do that to keep us safe. After that it was cool because he was showing me how to do stuff."

"He looks weird," Krissy remarked, and James shrugged.

"He's all right."

"I wish I could go outside with you." Krissy reached up and pushed her damp hair up off of her forehead. "It's boring watching TV all day with Mrs. Harper."

James's laugh was tired. "Pulling weeds isn't much better."

Still, it had to be better than sitting on a stiff sofa all day, watching boring grown-up shows.

James took himself off to bed, so Krissy crawled under her covers and listened to the deep rumble of her father's voice coming through the floor. He had been on the phone all evening, calling everyone who might know where his wife was. As she was drifting off, she wondered why he even bothered. Their mother was never coming home.

The next morning, Krissy was up before her father came in to get her up. She could tell by the noises coming from across the hall that James was already up, too.

The sky was still dark, though a band of sunlight striped the horizon where the sun was dawning as Krissy and James rode to the Harper's farm. Mr. Harper met them at the house and this time ushered them into the kitchen, where a fresh box of kid's cereal waited on the table.

"Miss Pat's still asleep, so help yourselves, and then we'll see if we can't find something for you to do," he said. Krissy and James sat at the table and poured out their cereal while Mr. Harper walked their dad out.

It felt weird eating someone else's food in someone else's house. Krissy and James hurried through their breakfast and then Krissy took their bowls to the sink and washed up. Unlike yesterday, the kitchen was spotless, and the dirty dishes that had littered the sink and counter were gone. Krissy set their bowls and spoons on the empty drain board, then turned at the sound of someone entering the kitchen.

"We're cleaning out one of the hay barns today," Zach said from the doorway, Jeremy standing behind him. Krissy could tell he was talking to James. "I hope you brought some muscles with you."

James shrugged and then nodded while Krissy made a face. Zach caught her expression.

"Getting sick of television all day?" he asked, smiling.

"It's fine...I guess," Krissy answered.

"You can help me if you want," Jeremy said. "We have an old chicken coop that we need to clean out. It's not hard, just a little dirty."

Krissy gave him a nod and an awkward smile. She and James followed the two men out.

The chicken coop wasn't as much a coop as it was an actual barn. Krissy imagined a cute, tiny little cottage where chickens sat in sweet little nests to lay their eggs. Where Jeremy took her was a long building with rows and rows of empty cages that sat on top of pans that had a hole at the back for the egg to roll out and down to a well at the front of the cage. Above that was another well that looked like it had held feed.

Jeremy handed Krissy a mask and a hand broom and instructed her to start sweeping the cages. By noon, she had all the cages clean and a huge pile of old feed peppered with chicken poop at the end of the barn. Together they bagged up the sweepings and then Krissy took off her mask and wiped the sweat from her forehead.

"You did a good job," Jeremy said, and to Krissy it sounded like he was trying to be nice so she smiled her thanks. She looked out across the farmyard and found James was pulling piles of old hay out of one of the other barns with Zach. They looked like they were having fun. Zach was saying something that had James smiling, and for some reason it made her angry that they looked like they were actually having fun. She wondered why James got to go with Zach while she was stuck with weird Jeremy. Zach looked strong, like he could protect her, while Jeremy just looked sick. If the kidnapper showed up, she was a goner.

"You know you don't have to worry, right?" Jeremy said, as if reading her mind. Krissy looked over at him as he leaned against the door-frame. "Nothing's going to happen, OK?"

Krissy wondered how he could know something like that but was grateful for the reassurance. She smiled and nodded.

"OK."

Jeremy smiled back at her and for once looked much less weird than before.

"Let's go get you some lunch," he said and then walked out of the barn.

While they had been working in the chicken barn, the sky had grown dark with clouds. They hurried to the house as fat drops of rain peppered the dusty farmyard below their feet. In the kitchen, Mrs. Harper was up and almost dressed in an old housecoat, her pendulous breasts swaying freely underneath. Krissy was pretty sure Mrs. Harper was naked underneath the thin cotton. She looked away and saw that James too had noticed and was trying to look anywhere else.

"Have a seat," Mrs. Harper said slowly. "I made sandwiches and soup. I think it's going to rain."

Krissy and James obeyed and took a seat at the table. Zach sat next to James and continued their conversation while Jeremy leaned against the counter and frowned. Krissy's stomach rumbled with hunger. Cleaning the barn had taken a lot out of her. She was looking forward to soup and sandwiches, but her enthusiasm turned to dismay when Mrs. Harper set a plate piled with burnt grilled cheese sandwiches in front of them, followed by bowls of cold canned tomato soup. Krissy could smell the sweet perfume of alcohol comingling with the stench of burnt bread and tinned soup.

Jeremy made a sound of disgust and moved to intercept his mother.

"Here. I'll do the rest," he offered, taking the spoons from her hand. "Why don't you go rest now?"

Mrs. Harper gave him a weak smile and nodded, then slowly left the room.

"Wow, that looks gross," Zach tried to joke. Jeremy ignored him and searched the cabinets and fridge for something else to eat.

"I think she used up the last of all the normal food we have," Jeremy said, slamming the refrigerator door. "There's nothing else here."

"How about I make a run to McDonald's?" Zach offered, and Krissy perked up. They didn't get fast food often, so when they did, it was a real treat. "James, you want to go with me?" Zach continued, and Krissy deflated—even more so when James nodded and got up.

155

"Cheeseburger and fries OK?" Zach asked her, and she nodded, still hoping he would ask her to go along. He smiled instead and ruffled her hair on his way out, James following right behind him.

Krissy watched as Jeremy's frown deepened, then frowned herself when he left the kitchen right after them. She sat and stared at the failed lunch and wondered what she was supposed to do. She could hear the television blaring in the other room but didn't really want to go in there. Instead, she stood and cleared the table, throwing away the burnt sandwiches and pouring the cold soup down the drain, then washed and dried the dishes. By the time she was done, James and Zach were back with rain-spattered bags of food.

Lunch was weird and uncomfortable, with Zach making overly cheerful conversation with James while Krissy sat there quietly. Jeremy hadn't returned and, from her seat, she could see him crossing the farmyard outside.

When they were done, Zack took James back out to finish their work on the barn, leaving Krissy alone again in the kitchen. She could see out the window that it was raining harder. She really didn't want to go outside, so she wandered into the living room, where Mrs. Harper sat snoring on the couch in front of some show about people who work on a boat. Someone had turned the volume down to the point where Krissy had to strain to hear it over the rain. With nothing else to do, she took a seat at the far end of the sofa and tried to watch, but the rain and boredom took their toll on her and soon she was asleep.

It wasn't until she felt someone shaking her that Krissy awoke. Bleary-eyed, she looked up and saw Jeremy looming over her.

"Your dad's here," he said quietly. Krissy nodded her understanding and stood. Mrs. Harper still slept at the other end of the sofa, so she carefully maneuvered past her to the door, where her father stood dripping water. She could hear the percussion of rain on the roof and felt the weight of the humidity in the warm, wet air. James stood just behind him, similarly soaked as if he'd just come in from outside himself.

Krissy took her place next to her father as he shook hands with Mr. Harper, and then the three of them ran for the car under a crash of thunder. By the time they drove away, Krissy was as wet as James. She stared out at the Harper's farm as Zach waved good-bye from the barn. James was smiling and waving back, and for some reason it annoyed Krissy. She wanted to ask him when they became such good friends but kept her mouth shut instead.

The rain was coming down in buckets by the time they drove the short distance to the Shepherd house. Krissy and James ran in behind their father, then shivered in the kitchen while he pulled towels out of the closet in Naomi's room. Krissy and James toweled off, then sat at the table where their father had dropped a bucket of fried chicken. As much as she loved fast food as a treat, Krissy missed Grandma Naomi's cooking and wished everything could go back to the way it was before Mason went missing.

Krissy daydreamed that Grandma Naomi and her mother were sitting at the table with them. It was an idealized daydream, with Ellen Shepherd laughing at something Krissy had said and Grandma Naomi able to talk. But it was beautiful nonetheless and she was lost in it when she heard her name.

"...and Krissy never does it," James was saying. "Besides, I was outside working all day while she got to watch TV all afternoon."

Krissy's father stood by the back door, shaking his head even as James was making his argument. Krissy had no idea what they were arguing about, but it sounded like something James really didn't want to do.

"When was the last time you washed a dish, James?"

Krissy thought that was a good point. She did all the washing up and almost all of the cooking...if you considered making bowls of cereal and peanut butter toast cooking. She could tell from James's expression that their father had made his point, but he continued to argue.

"But it's pouring out there," James began.

"And that's why I'm asking you to do it now before you go upstairs and dry off. It'll just take a minute and the can is full. Trash comes tomorrow. If it doesn't go out then it'll just pile up until next week."

Krissy finally got it. It was James's job to take out the trash and drag it to the end of the driveway so it could be picked up. She didn't blame him for not wanting to do it. She was soaked just running from the car to the house. She wouldn't want to go all the way to the end of the driveway, either.

"Ugh," James grunted, then pushed his chair back and stood. Their father handed him the kitchen trash and an umbrella, which James accepted reluctantly as he went out.

Krissy cleaned up the dinner dishes and the rest of the kitchen, then went upstairs to shower and change for bed.

She had just pulled her shirt over her wet hair when she heard her father call up the stairs.

"James?"

Krissy didn't think twice about it and pulled her pajama shorts on. The sound of the rain on the roof above her made her eyes droopy. She knew she'd be falling asleep quickly tonight.

"James?" her father called again.

Krissy stepped into the hall and looked at James's open door, then glanced in the bathroom next to it.

"He's not up here," she called down.

Her father didn't answer. Instead she heard footsteps run across the wood of the living room and the front door bang open.

"JAMES," she heard her father shout from outside. Krissy suddenly felt sick to her stomach. She took deep gulps of air, trying to fight the wave of nausea that threatened to bring up her dinner, then flew down the stairs and out the front door into the rain. In the distance she could see her father running down the driveway to the road. Despite her bare feet, Krissy followed, torrents of rain soaking her through in seconds.

"JAMES," her father bellowed, and then he stopped ahead of her and looked down. Unaware that the gravel had cut her feet, blood dotting every footstep for a second before the rain washed it away, Krissy slowed when she saw what her father was staring at. The trash can James had been pulling was tipped over onto the road, garbage littering the blacktop. Beside it, swaying in the gusts of wind that drove the rain sideways, lay the umbrella, crushed and torn. Only a single spine stood straight, the ripped nylon flapping in the wind.

This time it was her house that was filled with sheriff's deputies and men in navy-blue jackets stamped FBI. One of them had introduced himself to her, but she couldn't remember his name. She could remember the questions he asked, because he kept asking the same questions over and over again. They sounded different, but they were pretty much the same thing, and Krissy kept giving him the same answer. She didn't know where her brother could be except that he was probably with the kidnapper. Krissy couldn't consider the fact that he might be dead already, so she thought about her mother instead and wondered why no one was trying to find her to tell her James was missing.

The man interviewing Krissy had stepped away to speak to another man in a blue jacket. Someone had turned on the television, though the sound wasn't on. Its light illuminated the room, colors painting the walls as the image changed. Someone had put it on the weather channel and the screen glowed green. Krissy looked around and saw the house was filled with police. Out the window she could see men in bright-orange vests standing in the rain like they were having a meeting. Mr. Harper was with them, as were Zach and Jeremy. Mr. Harper seemed to be explaining something to one of the FBI guys, then pointed off in the direction of his farm. As Krissy watched, the men formed a line, switched on flashlights, and set off through Mr. Harper's corn. Behind her she could hear her father being interviewed by another FBI guy. His voice sounded strange, so she turned to look. Her expression turned stricken. She'd never seen her father cry before.

When she opened her eyes, Krissy couldn't remember falling asleep, but at some point she must have and someone had put her in her bed. Even though it was morning, the sky was dark. It was still raining, but not as hard as it had the night before. Krissy sat up and yawned, then remembered that James was still missing. Tears burned her eyes and she dropped her face into her hands and let herself cry. She didn't look up until her door opened. Her father stood in the doorway. He looked as awful as Krissy felt.

"I need you to get dressed, OK? I'm going to take you over to stay with Miss Pat while I go with the deputies."

"Where are you going?" Krissy asked, terrified that her father was leaving her.

"I'm going to help with the search party. Now that it's light, we'll be able take a better look around."

Krissy didn't see the point. If Mason, Justice, Clinton, and Minor weren't hidden in the corn, James certainly wasn't going to be there either. She kept her mouth shut, though, and pulled some clean clothes out of her drawer.

Downstairs Mr. Harper waited in the kitchen. He smiled when Krissy followed her father in.

"I can take her over there," he offered, and Krissy hoped her father would decline—but to her dismay, he nodded and thanked Mr. Harper. When her father kneeled in front of her and opened his arms, Krissy leaned into him and closed her eyes. More than anything she wanted her world to right itself, for James to be home, for her mother, even as mean as she was, to come back. For everything to be as it was. When she opened her eyes she looked at her father and knew that nothing was ever going to be the same again. Her father was making her promise something but Krissy had stopped listening. Instead she nodded, promising something and nothing, then followed Mr. Harper out.

The farm was surprisingly deserted and Krissy assumed everyone was out looking for James. Mr. Harper led Krissy into the house and settled her in the kitchen where milk, cereal, and a bowl were already waiting.

"Now you stay put here, OK? This the safest place for you right now," he said, then left. This time Mrs. Harper didn't even pretend to be interested in keeping her company. She made a brief appearance as Krissy was eating, then left right after refilling her coffee cup from a bottle tucked at the back of the pantry. Krissy heard the TV go on, but when she went into the living room, no one was there. She guessed she was expected to spend another day in front of the television, and the prospect was depressing. Instead, she sat on a small wooden bench in front of the window and watched the row of orange vests making their way through the fields on the far side of the farm.

By lunch, no one had come in and Mrs. Harper still hadn't emerged from wherever she was in the house. Krissy went into the kitchen and found some peanut butter and bread. There wasn't any milk left, so she drank tap water with her sandwich. When she was done she cleaned up her mess and stepped back into the living room. The rain was coming down harder again, and watching the volunteers creeping in the distance, she hoped they wouldn't give up. She sat and stared out at nothing, her mind numb to anything but the thought that her family was shrinking and there wasn't anything she could do about it.

By the late afternoon, Krissy's neck hurt from leaning against the window and her butt hurt from the hard wood of the bench. The house felt empty, and Krissy suddenly felt afraid. The rain had continued and dark had come early. From the corner of her eye, she saw Zach walking across the farmyard. Wanting some kind of company, Krissy got up and walked to the front door to call for him. But by the time she got the door open, Zach had disappeared into the barn across the way. With unnecessary quiet, Krissy closed the door and went out into the rain. Halfway across the dirt yard she heard noises coming from the barn, then saw Zach emerge from a door on the side of the barn she hadn't seen before. He moved away from her so she followed at a trot, hoping to catch up before Mr. Harper realized she wasn't in the house. He looked like he was headed for an old leaning barn that had originally belonged to her great grandfather. Krissy figured he was going to search the barn, so she picked up her pace so she could reach him in time to help him.

She had almost caught up to him when she realized that it was Jeremy and not Zach that she had been following. Krissy stopped to turn back toward the house when she spotted Zach following Jeremy from the other side of the farm. Even though it was dark, she could make out his tall, thin form catching Jeremy near the barn, and it looked like he was angry. The two men started to argue. In the dark, Jeremy's flashlight was waving wildly, and then it steadied and moved away as if guiding Zach along the old barn.

Krissy paused for a moment and considered returning to the house, then turned and followed the two men as they made their way to a small door on the side of the barn that was still mostly standing. Inside she could hear Zach's voice, and he was definitely angry. It was dark in the barn, but a beam of light cut across the ceiling as if someone had dropped the flashlight on the floor. Krissy walked over to where she'd seen the light come from and realized there was a set of stairs in the floor with a small wooden door propped open and leaning against a pile of old machinery.

She jumped at the sound of Zach's voice. It sounded like he was right under her feet.

"What the fuck is this?"

Krissy strained to hear Jeremy's response but could only make out a word here and there. She crept forward and slowly descended the stairs. It was pitch black with only Jeremy's flashlight providing a break in the darkness. Krissy's nose wrinkled at the smell of wet wood, vegetable rot, and what smelled like poo.

"Now you have to love me again," Jeremy said. He sounded like he was going to cry and it made Krissy uncomfortable. He'd been nice to her when he didn't have to and she didn't want him to be upset. She stopped at the bottom of the steps and tried to make out where Zach and Jeremy actually were. The cellar seemed bigger than she'd imagined and it looked like Zach and Jeremy were at the very end behind the steps she'd just come down. Krissy took a step forward, then bumped into something sharp and complicated in the dark. She stopped and moved around it carefully and found a smooth section of wall to guide her to the end of the room.

"What are you talking about?"

"You stopped loving me and I know it's because they got in the way. Just like Kirk did."

At the sound of Kirk's name, Krissy stopped, her confusion mounting. Why were they arguing about someone who disappeared so long ago?

"I don't know what you're talking about."

"You do know. And you can't deny it. I saw you talking to him. I saw you with him. I know you loved him, but now you have to love me."

Krissy heard Zach chuckle, but it was a mean laugh. "Dude, it's about fucking...not love. You should know that. You liked it."

Krissy's eyes widened at the language. She only sort of knew what they were talking about, but the idea of it was so foreign to her that it made her head swim.

"That's not true. We were together because you loved me."

"I loved fucking you, Jeremy, but I didn't love you."

"Is that why you stopped? Because you didn't love me anymore?"

"Jesus, when did I ever tell you I loved you?"

"I know you did. I could tell whenever we were together. I just don't know what I did to make it stop."

"You got too *old*."

"That's not true."

"Is that why you did this? Because you thought I loved them? Are you crazy?"

"I'm not crazy..."

"Are you serious? Look around you, Jeremy. You're completely crazy."

"I'M NOT CRAZY."

Krissy saw the light swing wildly and then stop. She stared, her eyes wide, for caught in its beam was Jeremy trying to kiss Zach on the mouth. Krissy's mind tried to process what she was seeing and then the light swung again when Zach pushed Jeremy away.

"Get the fuck off of me, you fucking freak," Zach said.

Krissy couldn't see Jeremy's face, but she could hear him sob.

"Don't call me that. I love you. I never stopped loving you. Why can't you love me again?"

"Who could love a freak like you?" she heard Zach sneer.

Krissy froze as the flashlight cut a bright arc across the ceiling, then reversed itself to streak the dark as it came down fast. She heard a thick, wet thud, and then the light went swinging again. When it stopped the light was duller, and the only thing she could hear was heavy breathing. She was about to call out when a dark figure rushed past her and up the stairs, the light shining on the floor and disappearing up through the ceiling. She could tell by the crying that it was Jeremy. She was about to follow when the wooden ceiling thudded, sending the cellar into complete darkness.

Krissy stood still and listened but couldn't hear anything but thick silence. When she was certain Jeremy wasn't coming back, she carefully moved in the direction of where she thought the stairs might be. She'd only moved a few inches when her toe caught on something in front of her, sending her crashing down on top of a pair of legs. Krissy realized she'd just fallen on top of Zach. She cried out and tried to push herself off, her hands slipping on the wet floor. She scooted on her backside until her back hit the wall behind her. Then she started to cry.

With the dark so penetrating, Krissy had no sense of time. All she knew was that she was stuck in a basement with Zach, who she was sure was probably dead, and she had no way of getting out. She wanted to wipe her eyes but her hands were wet with mud. She wiped them on the front of her shirt then pulled her shirt out of her shorts to clean them off better. She felt the hard plastic of her cell phone move against her leg as it started to fall out of her pocket. Krissy grabbed at it before it could get lost in the dark and pushed the button to make the screen light up.

For a moment the room was illuminated and Krissy cried out at the sight of Zach's bloody face. His eyes were open and staring, and in the brief second Krissy saw him, she knew he was dead. She turned away and with fumbling fingers tried to call her father but it went straight to voicemail. Krissy hung up and clutched the phone to her chest, tears in her eyes.

She didn't know it, but her father and Mr. Harper were frantically searching the house for her. Frank felt his phone buzz but accidently rejected the call trying to pull the phone out of his pocket.

Krissy wanted to cry. She wanted to be anywhere but in that stinking cellar. She wanted her father to come and get her and more than anything she wanted her brother back. She was so immersed in her misery that she didn't hear her phone at first. When the cheerful ring tone cut through the silence again, Krissy felt like her prayers had been answered. She pulled out her phone and frantically pushed at the buttons to answer it. She didn't see the shadow next to her that made the dark a little bit darker. She only felt him when he snatched her phone out of her hands. Krissy looked up and saw Jeremy's face bathed in the glow of her screen. Then he dropped the phone on the floor and stomped on it with his boot.

"I told you that you would be fine, didn't I?" he asked, but his voice sounded wrong. He had been crying before, but now he sounded like it was just another day, as if the last few hours had never happened. When he switched on the flashlight, she could see him in the halo of its glow. Krissy recoiled, thinking he would look terrifying, but he looked normal, almost kind, even though he was frowning. He was moving toward her when she found her voice.

"I want to go home," Krissy whispered. It was the only thing she could think of, and it seemed to give Jeremy pause.

"I know you do," he answered, and he looked so sad that Krissy felt horrible for having followed him.

"I'm sorry," she said.

Jeremy fell to his knees in front of her.

"It's not your fault," he said quietly. "Just close your eyes. This will be all over soon."

But Krissy couldn't look away. Jeremy was looming over her, the flashlight raised high. He paused a moment, and then before he could bring it down on her, another ring tone cut through the silence of the basement. Krissy watched Jeremy stand and look around in confusion. The room went silent for a moment, and then the ring tone went off again, this time from the far corner. Krissy stared as Jeremy rushed across the dirt floor toward the sound. Suddenly the basement was flooded with light, showing the piles of bones and rotted clothes that had lay for more than a decade in the dirt cellar. Behind Jeremy were more clothes, but they were newer, cleaner, and filled with the bodies of boys who had gone missing.

Krissy heard someone shout and then felt someone lifting her up and carrying her away from the scene of Jeremy trapped. She closed her eyes and heard a gunshot followed by a hot smell that almost masked the stench of death.

When she opened her eyes again, Krissy saw her father holding her tight while the men in blue jackets rushed them away from the barn. The rain had stopped, and the night was perfectly still. It was in this stillness that her father had heard James's phone.

TWENTY FIVE

Krissy sat and stared at the five coffins at the front of the church. Mason, Justice, Clinton, Minor...and James. She had been crying so much that her eyes could no longer make the tears she needed to wash away her grief. She glanced up at her father and saw that he too was all out of tears. She looked behind her to see if her mother had come, but there were too many faces staring back at her. The church was filled to capacity with people standing at the back and in the doorway. Beyond the crowd at the door, Krissy could see the green lawn at the front of the church filled with mourners and beyond that, far in the distance, a small black dot hanging from the branch of an old tree near a bridge that wasn't really a bridge. Krissy knew from the sway of that doll that the wind was blowing. But in the church it was silent. No one was speaking. No one coughed. They all just stood silently and waited. She turned back when the minister took his place at the pulpit but didn't care enough to listen. There wasn't anything he could say that would make the world OK again.

Other titles by K. Wiley Sider:
The Things That Fall Away
Solitary
Servant
Boy Toy, Book One of the Dead Husbands Series
Among the Missing

Learn more about the author at:
www.kwileysider.com
www.facebook.com/kwileysider

and on Twitter at:
@kwileysider

www.ingramcontent.com/pod-product-compliance
Lightning Source LLC
Chambersburg PA
CBHW071248130626
46556CB00003B/1219